KU-687-888

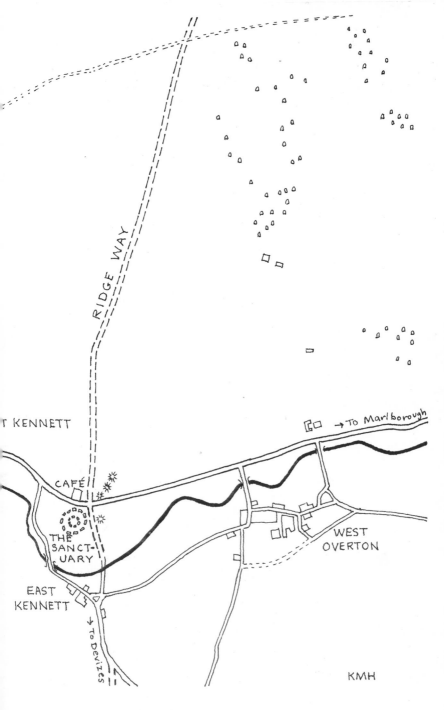

RIDGE WAY

T KENNETT

→ To Marlborough

CAFÉ

THE
SANCT-
UARY

WEST
OVERTON

EAST
KENNETT

→ To Devizes

KMH

BH 28 Graham Thwaites

NINE LOST DAYS

NINE LOST DAYS

by

MICHAEL HYNDMAN

London
GEORGE ALLEN & UNWIN
Boston   Sydney

© George Allen & Unwin (Publishers) Ltd, 1982
This book is copyright under the Berne Convention. No reproduction
without permission. All rights reserved.

George Allen & Unwin (Publishers) Ltd,
40 Museum Street, London WC1A 1LU, UK

George Allen & Unwin (Publishers) Ltd,
Park Lane, Hemel Hempstead, Herts HP2 4TE, UK

Allen & Unwin Inc.,
9 Winchester Terrace, Winchester, Mass 01890, USA

George Allen & Unwin Australia Pty Ltd,
8 Napier Street, North Sydney, NSW 2060, Australia

First published in 1982

British Library Cataloguing in Publication Data

Hyndman, Michael
  Nine lost days.
I. Title
823′.914 [F]   PR6058.Y/

ISBN 0-04-823221-1

Set in 10 on 11 point Century Schoolbook by
Rowland Phototypesetting Ltd, Bury St Edmunds, Suffolk
and printed in Great Britain by Biddles Ltd, Guildford, Surrey

For Sophie Josephine,
James Benedict and, of course, T Rexy Pooh.

CONTENTS

INTRODUCTION

Dawn. Midsummer's Day, year 17, eclipse cycle 335. Three hundred and thirty-five cycles, that is, since people (humans and the others) had come back to the Downs in the mud and slush of the early post-glacial years. By modern chronology 2250 BC.

Two figures were sitting on a hilltop looking at the sunrise. There was mist in the shallow valley below. Behind them was a low mound of chalk, lined and reinforced with massive upright rocks. In front, about a mile to the east, the next hilltop had broken through the mist to reveal the outline of a large circular thatched building. From its centre a point of reddish light shone at slow and regular intervals.

They were talking in low voices. Both were fairly tall, slim, fair and green-eyed. They wore nondescript brownish trousers, shirts and cloaks. A certain resigned, self-mocking manner marked their expressions and their speech.

'So they've finally decided to close this Transfer Station,' said one, 'I suppose it's definite this time?'

'Looks like it,' replied the other, 'they've started their rituals and all that. Circles it'll be from now on. Probably the same everywhere. Our clever human friends over there' – he nodded towards the hilltop opposite – 'have really gone overboard on this Pi 3 idea. They want to scrap all the Series I Transfer Stations. Pity. They were built to last. And I'm not all that happy about this stone circle technology anyway.'

His companion sniffed dismissively. 'Don't be a stick-in-the-mud; you know as well as I do that circles work much better than long barrows. Their time/space interfaces are already a whole quantum jump better than those of the old Transfer Stations. The Pi 3 effect still hasn't been maximised. Those scientists over at Durrington are on to something really big, and they know it. Give them a few years and they'll have a network of stations that'll get us anywhere and anywhen.'

The other smiled and shrugged. 'I suppose you're right,' he admitted, 'but circles are absolute nightmares to modulate, especially if they run on solar energy. A couple of earth tremors and you'd be in real trouble – or even a shift in the earth's axial inclination. Remember what happened to Finky Snid when Transfer Station 2 at New Grange drifted off synch? He'd got himself all kitted up for a holiday on the balmy shores of the Tethys Ocean – about forty million years ago, that is – forgot to lock the controls properly, and found himself materialising on a nunatak in a force ten blizzard. Surrounded by inquisitive woolly mammoths too. The rescue service had to chip him out of a block of ice when they eventually located him at about 80,000 years before present. Lucky for him he's immortal. But it could be you next time, Mar Ten, old friend.'

'That doesn't prove much,' observed the latter patiently. 'New Grange may have a circle but it's also equipped with a standard chamber backup facility. Solar-powered too, with a midwinter alignment. They tend to be a bit slap-happy about maintenance standards over there in Ireland. And Boan should have known better than to let a ham-fisted idiot like Snid go tinkering around with her best and most beautiful station. I bet she gave him a dose of Mode 3 hell afterwards.' He shivered and changed the subject. 'Anyway, how's our own lovely local goddess taking the news?'

'Quite well, when I saw her last. She was keeping to Mode 1; says it works best with humans – you know, the sweet-maiden-in-distress approach: "Please help me, you great strong men, I'm only a weak little sprite." Lumbering idiots. They usually respond by beating their chests and heaving whole mountains around. Look at the hill they made for her' – he glanced to his left, where in the vale a huge cone-shaped mass of white chalk was emerging from the mist. 'Mind you,' he added reflectively, 'she switched quickly enough into Mode 3 when the first synchroherence tests failed. Put the fear of death into them; and into me too, for that matter. But she's got a lot to thank the humans for: two of the best Transfer Stations in the world; the Hill, for what it's worth; and now they've promised her a circle to end all circles. A genuine triple three – one huge circle with two smaller ones inside it in synchroherence with sub-installations at Lios and Brodgar. A hundred and twenty-five yards across – the *small* ones that is – heaven alone knows the size of the main circle.'

Mar Ten seemed impressed. 'So it really is all happening here; with that sort of power her ladyship will be all set to jump right up to the Edge of Time. Boan and Sorvi won't be too happy about that. I've never met a goddess yet who wasn't as prickly as a hedgehog over matters of personal prestige. Those bright boys and girls Sorvi's got working for her down Stonehenge way will probably be only too keen to try to go one better if she asks them to. Triple elliptical interlocks on midsummer dawn, they were talking about when I was there last. And ancillary inputs from just about

2

everything else: moon up, moon down, equinoxes, eclipses, stars, midwinter. The lot. They've even asked me to help design their interdimensional silicon circuits.'

'I reckon they're overdoing it all,' reflected the other. 'All right, humans have physical power, a lot of determination and mental reflexes that make our own look sluggish, to say the least. But this trend towards materialism is turning them into a lot of insensitive grabbers. They've already lost telepathy and psychokinesis, their magic is pretty hopeless – they were quite good at *that* even during the Ice Age – and they seem to spend all their time battering away at nature rather than in co-operating with her. If they don't watch out they'll end up as a bunch of wealthy savages. Look at what's happening in Mesopotamia and Egypt: slavery, wars, plagues. There aren't many of *us* left down there. Ishtar and Isis aren't too happy about it all, despite all those ziggurats and pyramids. Things will be the same here once they organise their metal technology, mark my words. It'll mean the end of symbiosis.'

Mar Ten grinned. He didn't seem at all worried by his friend's pessimism. 'Well, there's always the rest of the space-time continuum. A thousand million years are plenty for me. I can never really comprehend why so many immortals get hooked on the Quaternary. Now we've developed the Long Leap the whole of the palaeozoic and mesozoic eras are open to us. Give me dinosaurs rather than humans any time; they're much more sophisticated creatures and even the clever ones don't get crazy ideas about organic self-sufficiency. What's more, the weather during the Cretaceous is a sight better than it is here at the tail end of the Ice Age. That's where I'm off to now. I need a holiday after all those abstruse Pi 3 mathematics that I've been doing lately. Give my respects to her ladyship when you see her.'

He glanced at the round house across the valley. While he had been speaking the flashes of light had quickened into a continuous beam which had locked on to the mound behind them, illuminating it with a faint reddish glow. Mar Ten stood up, turned around and approached the mound's facade. There was a gap in the centre of the massive sarsen rocks. Behind the gap was a small forecourt and beyond that a dark, cave-like entrance. Mar Ten gazed intently into the opening for a moment; then he went in. Inside he could see very little, but with an assured step he walked about ten paces forward and then ducked into a small chamber let into the left side. The passage itself widened and came to an end in a blank wall of stones. One of these, larger than the rest, was already fluorescing dully. Mar Ten sat down and waited. After about five minutes the quality of the light around him began to change. The diffuse red

3

glow faded out and was replaced by a concentrated ray of energy – sensed rather than seen – that drove into the stone at the end of the passage. Its colour began to shift through the spectrum from red to yellow, yellow to green, green to blue, and then to a violet of such combined faintness and intensity that he had to shield his vision. He sat back in the chamber and began to count. When he reached 81 he cautiously poked his head out and surveyed the stone through half-closed eyes. It no longer glowed. But its texture had changed to that of the silvery, plastic form of an underwater bubble, reflective and mobile at the same time. He carefully stepped out into the passage and advanced to the shimmering interface. About a yard in front of it, he stopped, bowed and said in a firm voice: 'Your ladyship, Mar Ten of the Sidhe requests transfer. The Statute has been observed; the gate is open.' Without waiting for a reply he walked forward into the quivering barrier. And vanished through it. For perhaps a second the surface continued to reflect in random patterns the faint daylight from the entrance. Then with an audible 'pop' it reverted to its original luminous stony appearance. Transfer Station 1 had returned to its stand-by phase.

DAY ONE

A dull, wet afternoon in late October. The school bus swung across the A4 road into a lay-by, braked, skidded and rebounded gently off the kerb before stopping. Miss Piercy grabbed the luggage rack above her head and hauled herself up. 'Here we are,' she cried with a forced brightness. 'Now listen, everybody, *please*.'

She waited for about twenty seconds and continued: 'At Avebury we saw the largest prehistoric stone circle in the country. That big mound just behind us on our left is Silbury Hill, the largest artificial hill in Europe, I think. And on our right is the West Kennett Long Barrow, where the prehistoric people used to bury their chiefs. Can you see it, along the skyline at the top of the ridge?'

A series of noncommital grunts signified that her pupils either could or couldn't. A sharp downpour of rain at Windmill Hill, followed by continuous drizzle and the high prices of refreshments at their previous stop, had done much to dissipate whatever enthusiasm forms 5S and 6L might have felt towards the prehistoric monuments of Ancient Britain. Some of the more resilient pupils wiped the condensation off the windows with their sleeves and peered owlishly in one or other of the directions indicated by their teacher. Others chewed, conversed, giggled or surreptitiously drank from cans or bottles. Miss Piercy glanced quickly around and continued – more loudly but also rather nervously – 'I want two groups. One's to come with me to look at Silbury Hill, which is the largest prehistoric mound in the world, I think. The others can go up to the long barrow. Don't forget your clipboards and worksheets. Everybody out, please.'

On cue, the driver pressed the pneumatic door release. He grinned at his passengers and picked up a copy of the *Sun*. The doors swung open and the children jostled each other reluctantly out of the coach.

Once on the path Ben Jameson looked quickly around. The others seemed to be crowding towards the rear wheels of the coach. Ahead, a signpost to West Kennett Long Barrow pointed across a muddy and waterlogged meadow beyond which a ploughed and equally muddy slope rose into the middle distance. Silbury Hill, the obvious objective of everyone else, lay only a few hundred yards back along the road.

Ben felt for the hard outlines of the two illicit cans of pale ale in his anorak pockets and made for the footpath gate. As he opened it he heard a familiar voice calling him. Without pausing he shouted 'Go away, will you, you horrible female', and slammed the gate shut. But it was too late. With his sister Josie it was always too late, he reflected glumly.

'Such unfraternal sentiments only conceal a warm and generous nature,' she observed brightly, climbing the gate and jumping down beside him. 'Need I remind you, dearest brother, that it was my money you borrowed to buy that booze with in Marlborough. How about sharing it?'

Ben surveyed his sister with mingled exasperation and respect. Josie had, at a young and relatively tender age, acquired the knack of disarming opposition. Adults (including even Miss Piercy) usually melted before her ready smile and sunny nature. Contemporaries usually appeared susceptible to her generous spirit (sweets shared, cuddly toys, robust humour). It seemed that only he (Ben reflected bitterly) could discern the calculating shrewdness behind it all. Mentally he resigned a can – or perhaps only half a one – knowing from experience that any too violent attempt to discourage Josie would lead to her calling a gaggle of her friends over.

Alone, therefore, the two of them tramped through the boggy field. The path was quite a good one, leading down towards a bridge over a small stream and then veering left through another gate and right again up the hill towards the barrow.

A herd of black and white Friesian cattle watched them incuriously. Josie unzipped the centre pocket of her anorak, pulled out her radio-cassette player (a present from last birthday) and switched on. Radio 1 howled out over the peaceful dampness of the countryside. 'Turn that racket off,' ordered Ben, and then compromised, 'or at least get something less horrible. Try Radio 3.'

Josie complied without argument and the Boomtown Rats faded, to be replaced by a burst of orchestral music. Slightly eerie, thought Ben, but at the same time powerful and full of movement. He didn't recognise it. 'Debussy,' said Josie, as though reproaching his ignorance, 'twelve-tone scale and all that. One of the Three Nocturnes. "Fêtes", I think.'

They came to the gate which opened into the enclosure containing the long barrow. Just inside was a notice giving basic information about the site, together with a plan. They gave it a cursory glance and then inspected the monument. To their right stood side

6

by side a row of massive stones. The end ones were relatively small, but in the centre was an imposing sarsen twelve feet or more high. Behind this facade rose the mound of the long barrow itself, stretching for a hundred yards along the ridge they had just climbed. Down below was the main road with their school bus clearly visible in the lay-by. Beyond the road the distinctive shape of Silbury Hill dominated the landscape. At its foot a group of figures in brightly coloured anoraks could be made out: the rest of the party. The view seemed remote and even unreal – rather as if it were on a television screen a long way off. The long barrow and its facade seemed to combine with the low grey sky above and – somehow – the Debussy music from Josie's radio-cassette to create their own dimension of time and space.

'Spooky, isn't it?' Josie's question brought Ben back to earth. He remembered his beer and followed his sister over to the barrow entrance. She was waiting for him in the little forecourt between the great centre stone of the facade and the cavernous opening to the tomb. She was looking a bit puzzled, Ben thought. 'What's the matter?' he asked, more loudly than he had intended; and then he realised the music could no longer be heard. 'Scared?'

Josie shook her head. 'Not really,' she frowned uncertainly, 'but my radio's faded. I put in new Duracells only yesterday. Perhaps it's all those rocks. I've turned it right up.' She held out the silent radio-cassette. Ben took it and retraced his steps. Immediately he passed beyond the facade the music crashed out at full volume, distorting the loudspeaker. He took a pace between the upright stones. The music died away.

'Hear that?' he called back over his shoulder. 'It must be the barrow damping out the radio signal. Rather sudden, though.' He moved the radio-cassette to and fro several times: silence – music – silence – music – more silence. There seemed to be a clear-cut but invisible barrier shutting off reception. Intrigued, he recrossed the forecourt, handed the set back to his sister and together they entered the passage.

Inside they could discern the shadowy tunnel leading into the mound. Two small chambers led off on either side and after about ten yards the passage widened and ended in a blank wall of stone. By now they could make out the outlines of the upright supporting rocks and the corbelled roof quite well. It felt cold and smelt damp. Water drops glistened and some of the stones were shiny with moisture.

Then someone spoke, quite distinctly. Both jumped as a surge of surprise and fright ran through them. Josie felt the hairs on the back of her neck rise; after a moment she relaxed a little and

7

laughed. 'It's only my radio,' she exclaimed in a tone of obvious relief, and switched it off to prove the point. She switched it on again, and the voice – that of a young woman – started talking almost immediately. Whoever it was sounded anxious. But the words meant nothing. They weren't English, French or German. The voice seemed to reach the end of its message. There was silence for a few seconds, and it began once more.

Ben, still feeling weak in the knees, leant on one of the stones for support. He slipped and nearly fell over when Josie exclaimed, 'I know what she's talking now – it's Latin.' Her voice was sharp with incredulity. Ben listened carefully. He had given up Latin – thankfully – in the third form, but one or two words still made sense.

'Ad portam ... pridie Kalendas Novembres' (where had he heard that phrase before?) and then the last words 'quosquos audientes oro et iubeo.' Ben knew what they meant: I beg and order whoever is listening ... 'How much of that did you get?' he whispered. 'Quite a lot,' replied Josie, who was taking Latin to O level.

But the voice began again. Still urgent in tone, it seemed to be addressing them directly. The third part of the message was in yet another language. A familiar on-the-tip-of-the-tongue sensation occurred simultaneously to both children as odd words began to make sense, only to be followed by sequences of near misses. It was like listening to someone speaking English, or something very like it, with a very strong West-Country accent. The word 'I' came over repeatedly, with a hint of 'ch' after it. But the language certainly wasn't German; individual words could be distinguished quite clearly, but together they meant nothing.

In the silence that followed they could hear each other breathing. Josie's fingers scrabbled over the switches of her radio-cassette, selected one and clicked it on. A faint humming began. 'I've put it on "record",' she whispered. The voice began once more. The words seemed the same, but the expression behind them a little more anxious. Ben and Josie listened to each of the three languages in turn, a resolution growing that they would have to do something to help. But what?

A shadow fell across the tomb's entrance. The spell was broken. 'Josie and Ben, are you hiding in there?' shouted someone. 'Miss P's doing her nut. There isn't time for the rest of them to come up here and she wants you to get back to the bus as soon as possible. Come on out, will you?'

Blinking, they emerged. One of their friends was looking curiously at them. 'Seen a skeleton, or something?' she asked.

8

'Come on, hurry back or else we'll be too late for the school buses.'

The three charged down the hill and across the field to the coach, Josie clutching her radio-cassette and Ben his still unopened cans of beer. Already the eerie world of the stone chamber had receded into unreality. Each step brought them further back to the familiar problems and routine of everyday life.

That evening Ben was concentrating his mind upon the intricacies of the Avogadro constant and its applications to chemistry when his sister came into the room carrying her radio-cassette. 'Out!' he said fiercely, without looking up. 'Get out. I've got a test tomorrow.'

But Josie was immune from the big brother gambit. 'Listen you pig,' she began, and having obtained her brother's attention if not his approval continued, 'I've been replaying that tape we recorded in the barrow today – the Latin part of it, at least. I think it was being transmitted by someone calling herself a *goddess*. Her name's Qenet – she pronounces it a bit differently from the river Kennet but it's almost the same. The Latin's quite easy in places, though it's not perfect. This is what I think she's saying.' Josie glanced at the sheet of notepaper she held in her hand:

> Ego Qenet sum, huius loci et fluminis dea
> I am Qenet, the goddess of this place and river
> Iuvanda sum
> I need help
> Ex altero mundo loquor
> I am speaking from the other world
> Meas terras hominesque in mundo medio rursus videre iamdiu volo
> For long I have wanted to see my lands and people in the middle
> world again
> Sed porta clausa est
> But the gate is locked.

Josie paused and frowned 'Now it becomes more difficult, but the gist of it seems to be:

> Ad portam aperiendam in hoc tumulum vesperi pridie Kalendas
> Novembres venire debetis
> To open the gate you should come into this mound on the
> evening of 31 October – that's tomorrow, in case you
> haven't realised –
> Lux magna et subita facienda erit
> A great and sudden light will have to be made
> ter et ter et ter – I just couldn't make this out for ages,
> but I *think* it must mean three times three times over

Quosquos audientes haec agere oro et iubeo
I pray and command whoever is listening to do these things.'

Having finished, Josie looked around Ben's room a little dif-
fidently. With its model aeroplanes and missiles, its bright posters
showing steam engines and supersonic aircraft, its litter of do-it-
yourself electronic equipment, science books and magazines, it
seemed an unlikely place for the two of them to be considering a
message out of the other world from someone who described herself
as a river goddess.

Or was it? Qenet – whoever she was – at least seemed re-
freshingly free of the twee mannerisms often affected by supernatural beings in fiction. A very practical and modern-sounding
goddess, Josie reflected, if indeed the whole thing wasn't a hoax.

Ben, who usually prided himself upon his detached scientific
scepticism, remained silent, moodily contemplating the radio-
cassette. He reached forward and took it from Josie, pressed the
fast rewind button, waited for the automatic stop to cut in, and
then pushed the replay switch. The voice came over just as he
remembered it: precise, carefully pronouncing each word and
clearly rather worried that the message would not be understood.
The first language still meant nothing to him, but the words of the
Latin version seemed quite distinguishable. And now that he had
Josie's translation the opening sentence of the third passage
suddenly began to make sense: 'I, Qenet, of this land and burn
goddess . . .'

'I played some of it to father,' broke in Josie. 'He reckons this
part's in Anglo-Saxon. He had to study the Dark Ages at university.' She ran out of the room without further explanation and
returned a few minutes later with a thick brownish book entitled
Stubbs' Select Charters from the beginning to 1307.

'Look,' she continued, opening it near the front, 'here's a law
dated 690 – they wrote "I" as "Ic" then, and that's just how Qenet,
or whoever she is, pronounces it. And see – she pointed to another
page – 'here's the word she uses in the bit about the light –
thriwa, thriwa", she says. That's thrice three times – sounds like a
tongue-twister, doesn't it? And another thing – father says the
first language sounds like Welsh, though he can't understand a
word of it.'

Ben spoke for the first time. 'I just can't make it out. It seems like
someone's having us on. But why? It's altogether too complicated
for a practical joke. Your mob never think of anything except
forging sloppy love-notes and then giggling. My lot are still at the
mercury fulminate stage. Good stuff, that,' he added reflectively.

10

'Scared old Piercy rigid when we put some cracker snaps under her desk last April Fool's Day. Thought she'd been mined. Pow!'

'Of course it's not a practical joke,' interrupted Josie quite indignantly. 'It sounds far too sensible for that. It might be a secret spy transmission, but who would want to send it in three different languages, especially if it's not coded?'

Ben dismissed the idea. 'Spies don't broadcast on Radio 3 frequency, or at speaking speed – unless they want to get caught. They have special high-speed transmissions. Read about them in one of John le Carré's books. Anyway, don't you remember the way the barrow blanked off incoming signals? Now that was *really* weird. But what does it all mean?'

'It means', said Josie with decision, 'that either someone's trying to make fools of us or it's a genuine request for help. If it's a joke, then whoever's behind it has a radio transmitter and has gone to a heck of a lot of trouble to have us on. But *I* don't think it's that. I think there's sufficient chance that it's real to make it worthwhile to go along with it. And it does make a change, doesn't it?'

'O.K.,' agreed Ben. 'So just what do we have to do? This Qenet person wants us to go up to the barrow tomorrow evening because she's been waiting to see her people and lands for a long time – about 1,500 years, in fact, if she thinks we're still speaking Anglo-Saxon. And to open what she calls the gate between our world and the other world we've got to do all this mumbo-jumbo with lights. What exactly is it she wants?'

'A great and sudden light . . . three times three times over,' read Josie. 'I suppose she means nine times in all. Three groups of three flashes – a sort of code, like the ones people use to open those automatic garage doors they were showing on *Tomorrow's World*,' she added, in a moment of inspiration.

'But why on 31 October, of all days?' queried Ben. He rose and went over to his desk, rummaged among the books and papers that covered its top, and extricated a diary from the litter. 'Let's see. Thirty-first of October . . . Hallowe'en. First of November . . . All Saints' Day. Here, wait a mo! Where are you going?'

For Josie had jumped up as though electrified and had charged headlong out of the room and down the stairs. Within a couple of minutes she was back.

'Now just shut up and listen for a bit.' She was looking through the index of a large black and gold coffee-table type book called *Folklore, Myths and Legends of Britain* which she had evidently just removed from the bookshelves below. She was very excited – all fingers and thumbs – but she eventually found the page she was seeking.

11

'I knew it, I knew it!' she exclaimed. 'Look – here's the answer to it all: page 23. "Timeless festivals remembered. The Celtic calendar, based on the agricultural and pastoral year, began on November 1, which our ancestors celebrated with the great festival of Samain . . .

' "Samain was believed to be a time when natural laws were suspended, and ghosts and demons roamed abroad. It was a time, too, when great fires were lit to ensure the renewal of life in the earth . . . This all-important day could not be ignored by the early Church, who rededicated the occasion to the saints in Heaven. It was instituted in AD 835 and called All Saints' Day. Traces of Samain still linger in Hallowe'en (All Saints' Eve – October 31) and its traditional associations with ghosts and witches." '

Josie looked in the index, found another page, and continued '"Hallowe'en is derived from the ancient festival of Samain, which on October 31 marks the eve of the Celtic new year. Samain was associated with burial mounds which were thought to be" ' – and at this point her voice went up half an octave – ' "entrances to the other world." That's it. The other world. "Ex altero mundo," the message says. That's where Qenet is. The long barrow must be one of the places where you can get from our world to hers. Samain's the best time to transfer from the other world into this one because the laws of nature are suspended then. All we've got to do is to provide the sequence of light flashes. It goes on here' – she tapped the book – 'about the great bonfires they used to light outside the barrows. I expect the flickering flames used to trigger off the opening of the gate. Don't you see, it really does make some sense. Hallowe'en, the long barrow, the light and the other world.'

She paused, and looked at Ben, enthusiasm conflicting with doubt in her mind as she recalled that her brother prided himself (sometimes a little priggishly) upon his logical and analytical approach to the problems of life. There didn't seem much room for all this mythological and romantic stuff in his view of the world.

Ben sat deep in thought for what seemed several minutes and then he began to speak in what Josie recognised as his best scientific-detachment tone of voice. 'You know, it's really quite possible. Theoretically, I mean. Several worlds can exist together in the same place. Even heavy elements like metals consist almost entirely of empty space with a few atomic particles scattered around. So there's plenty of *room* for this other world thing. Sort of interlocked with ours. That's why people say ghosts can walk through walls. They're supposed to exist in the same *space* as us, but in a different dimension.'

Josie had by now realised, rather to her surprise, that there was

12

not after all going to be a withering rejection of her ideas. But she was puzzled by Ben's explanation and by his acceptance of her opinion.

'Come downstairs a moment – I'll give you a demonstration of the kind of thing I mean,' said Ben, and led her into the living-room. He switched on the T.V. The screen lit up to show two cowboys smashing each other, and their immediate surroundings, up. 'U.S.A., western states, around 1880,' he explained unnecessarily. He pressed one of the channel selection buttons. The scene changed instantly: a group of men, dressed as clowns, were wheeling hoops along a narrow plank bridge over a water tank. Girls in bathing costumes were throwing artificial custard pies and trying to make them fall in. 'England, 1980,' commented Ben, and pushed another button: a familiar figure with pointed ears was speaking. 'It appears to be a Romulan ship, captain, headed for Rigel IV,' he said impassively as a sinister bat-like shape slid on to the screen. 'Outer space, about 500 years from now,' concluded Ben.

Josie resisted an impulse to tell him to keep it on. 'You see,' said Ben, 'all these different places and times seem to exist simultaneously on our T.V. set here. All you've got to do is switch on and select your programme. The long barrow could hypothetically be a receiver and all these flashing lights that Qenet – whoever she is – wants could be a way of activating it and tuning in from one dimension to another. You can transmit with as much power as you like but you won't get through unless someone switches on the set at the other end. I think we ought to give the whole thing a try; anyway, there's nothing worth watching on telly. Tomorrow's the 31st and we break up for half-term, so all we've got to do is organise a trip to the long barrow and work out how to create the special lighting effects Qenet wants. It should be a bit of a gas if nothing else. What we could do with is a disco strobe light, but even if we could borrow one we'd never get the power up there. The place must be about half a mile from the nearest electricity point.'

Ben's optimism had a paradoxically depressing effect upon Josie. His matter-of-fact scientific explanations seemed to wreck the rather cosy and fanciful world that she had half subconsciously been building up around the events of the day. Magic of the conventional kind she could understand and – almost – believe in. But Ben's prosaic interpretation of it all seemed a bit too cut-and-dried; not at all cosy – rather frightening, in fact. A space-age, science-fiction goddess? Visions of inimical bug-eyed monsters, Daleks, Klingons, Imperials and other extraterrestrial nasties came to her mind. The invasion of earth? Oh no!

She explained her fears to Ben, and at once began to feel better.

13

Put into words it all sounded trite and improbable. Space-age aliens would have powerful starships bristling with energy beams and disintegrators. They wouldn't need the help of ordinary people like herself and her brother. The opening sequence of *Star Wars* came back to her. Nor would they speak in Welsh (or whatever it was), Latin and Anglo-Saxon. She picked up her radio-cassette and impulsively switched it on once more. Reassurance flooded back as the now familiar voice began once again. No arrogant and bloodthirsty alien could talk like that, she told herself. The voice sounded too appealingly human.

Their father entered the room in time to hear the last sentences of the trilingual message. 'Yes, that's Anglo-Saxon all right,' he confirmed. 'I had to learn some of *Beowulf* at college – but that's not part of it. Is that why you borrowed my book? What's it all about, anyway?'

Josie looked at Ben; Ben looked at Josie. They both realised that a moment of decision had arrived.

'Well Dad,' began Ben, 'it's like this.' And he gave what seemed to his sister an admirably matter-of-fact account of what had happened that afternoon in the barrow. He even mentioned the beer. 'We don't really know what to make of it,' he concluded. 'It's a bit scary, but we can't help thinking that we ought to do something about it.'

Their father replayed the whole message without comment; then he called their mother, who came in with a hair-dryer in her hand and muttered darkly that whatever it was, it had better be worth listening to.

'Well,' she said when she also had heard Qenet's broadcast, 'there must be *something* behind all this; perhaps someone's killing themselves laughing at you. Someone with a walkie-talkie. But it is a bit of an adventure, isn't it? I suppose you three romantics want to go over to the barrow tomorrow just to see if anything happens. But don't be too surprised if one of your more imaginative friends jumps out at you dressed in a Dracula outfit.'

The upshot of the discussion which followed was that all four of them should drive over to the barrow at about half past five on the following day. Josie (to the secret relief of Ben) firmly refused to go too long after it had become really pitch-black. Their parents would wait in the car at the lay-by while Josie and Ben, armed with an assortment of torches and a rounders bat (just in case) would walk up to the barrow. If nothing unusual happened (and that is what they all expected) they could drive into Marlborough and cheer themselves up at one of the pubs there. Only one problem remained.

14

'By the way,' queried their father, 'how are you going to rig up these nine lights? The whole thing may sound a bit potty but at least you ought to go through the right procedure, don't you think?' He gave his Frankenstein monster imitation, baring his fangs and rolling his eyes, and stalked out of the room. Mother winked and followed.

'He's got a point, you know,' admitted Ben. 'A strobe set would do fine, but, like I said, it's just not on.'

Josie assumed a pose of tolerant condescension and said nothing. She reckoned that it couldn't fail to irritate Ben and she was right. 'O.K., brain-pot, I suppose you've got it all worked out.' He seized a cushion and threw it half-heartedly at her.

She dodged. 'Flash bulbs, goon. My camera takes a twelve-bulb flash-bar. Leave the film out, set it on "flash" and press the shutter release. No problem if you're a genius.' And Josie, knowing from experience that Ben's rejoinder was almost sure to be a violent one, blew him a raspberry, ran up to her room, slammed the door and bolted it.

DAY TWO

It was a sceptical and vaguely self-conscious group that piled into the family car at a quarter to five on the following day, Hallowe'en. The Citroën GS estate (new-second-hand and bright orange in colour) bore them along the A4 through the murk of the autumn evening. They stopped at the lay-by. The engine cut out and for a moment no one moved. Outside it had begun to drizzle.

'Got everything?' their mother asked. Josie grabbed her camera and checked that the new flash-bar was in her anorak pocket. She had also decided, at the last minute, to bring her radio-cassette. Ben carried an imposing portable searchlight with a red flashing dome and his pockets contained an assortment of less powerful torches. They opened the doors and got out. 'Don't forget this,' shouted their father, passing the rounders bat through the open window. Josie took it thankfully; it gave her a real feeling of security.

The two of them walked to the field gate. Already the car was disappearing into the fuzzy gloom. The beam from Ben's torch faded into the twilight just ahead of them. They crossed the stream, reached the second gate and began to climb the slope up to the long barrow. The narrow path was easy to follow, though a bit slippery from the rain, and Ben's torch became more effective as they neared the final gate into the enclosure round the barrow.

'Look,' said Ben, breaking a long silence, 'someone's dumped a load of wire netting and stakes over there by the notice.' They examined the tidy pile of fencing material and then made for the barrow entrance. Ben handed his sister a torch and together they hunted around the massive stones. There was no sign of anyone. The whole site was deserted. There was no possible excuse for delaying their entry into the silent black passageway. Josie tightened her grip on the bat as Ben pointed the searchlight beam into the gap between the stones. They edged forward into the forecourt. Nothing moved. Ben shone the light into the entrance. The beam lit up the interior. It looked cold, damp and empty. He went in, placed the lamp on the floor, and angled the light up to the roof. At once much of the chamber was illuminated with a yellowish glow. He shone one of his other torches into each of the four small side chambers. They were empty.

16

'Nothing here; you can come in,' he whispered. He sounded relieved. Josie didn't know whether to be glad or not. In the reflected brightness of the searchlight she even felt a little disappointed. She stood uncertainly near the end of the passage where it widened out into the end chamber.

'Get a bloody move on, will you?' hissed Ben from a side-chamber on the right. Josie switched on her radio. Boney M's latest number came blaring out. She turned the tuning-knob as far as it would go. 'Delta Tango Two, Delta Tango Two,' intoned a deadpan voice. 'Proceed to the Wiltshire Poacher public house, where an affray has been reported.' Josie switched off. Again she experienced a slight sensation of disappointment. Everything seemed too *normal*. She placed the radio-cassette carefully behind the lamp and took out her camera. She was surprised how calm she felt. She jammed the flash-bar in its socket, pointed it at the end wall of the chamber, switched off the light, and pressed the release button of the camera. A dazzling blue-white glare filled the whole tomb. 'One,' she counted, wound on, and pressed the button again. 'Two, Three.' She began to find that the alternation of intense light and pitch darkness was making her dizzy and wished she had had the sense to rest her back on one of the upright stones. But she couldn't stop now. 'Four, Five, Six; Seven, Eight, Nine.' She almost choked on the last number.

Ben switched on his torch. Still half blinded, Josie could just about see enough to reach out and steady herself on the nearest rock. She closed her eyes tightly for a few seconds to try to drive away the residual glare of the flashes, and then opened them. Even now she couldn't see much. Just enough to make out the space in front of her. It was empty. For the third time that evening Josie felt a twinge of disappointment – mixed, however, with relief. 'Oh, well. Back to the drawing-board,' she said.

No reply came from Ben. Josie turned towards him. He was still just inside the side-chamber to her right, his face showing in the back-reflection of his torch. His eyes were wide open and he seemed to be trying to say something. For a split second Josie felt panic-stricken, and then anger took over. 'Don't you *dare* try to scare me, you wretch. Stop messing around *at once* or I'll belt you one.' In an access of rage she snatched up the rounders bat and stepped threateningly towards her brother. Her approach seemed to bring him back to reality. He grasped her shoulders and turned her, protestingly, round. Josie froze. Standing in the corner of the end chamber, not three yards from her, was a woman.

'She came through the rock. She just stepped right through it' whispered Ben hoarsely. 'And she hasn't shifted since.'

17

The newcomer was so near that neither of them dared move. For a chaotic minute or so they surveyed the figure in front of them. She was reassuringly human. Tallish, blonde, wearing a hooded emerald-green silk dress embroidered with intertwined animals in gold. Hair plaited, eyebrows dark; very long, almost artificial-looking eyelashes, rosy cheeks. Red nails, crimson mocassin-type shoes, gold twisted bracelets on both arms. Her eyes were closed, and she seemed absorbed in thought.

Abruptly she opened her eyes, saw them, and smiled. 'Hello,' she said, 'I'm Qenet. Q – E – N – E – T. Sorry I couldn't speak more sooner. Had to adjust to your language. It's an evolved kind of Anglo-Saxon, isn't it? Many, many thanks indeed for activating the Transfer Station. I thought that I would never be able to get through. What are your names, please, and who are you?'

Her speech had a slight lilt. Gaelic, perhaps, thought Ben, or perhaps Irish. It certainly wasn't upper-class English or even West-Country. Qenet smiled again. 'Not used to Transfer, I suppose. I expected elves not humans. Inside of barrows usually *geis* to humans.' She frowned. 'Taboo', she pronounced doubtfully, 'means the same in your language. Funny word. Exotic.' She looked in a faintly puzzled way at the torch which Ben was holding. 'Surely that's elf-light,' she exclaimed. 'You *are* human, aren't you. Homo sapiens sapiens. Not half-*sidhe* or something like that?'

Ben shuffled in a self-conscious way. 'Well,' he began, but Josie interrupted him. 'Yes, we're human. I'm Josie and sixteen. He's Ben and seventeen. My brother. We received your message on my radio and did as you asked. So here we are.'

'Electromagnetic reception and amplification; you *have* come a long way,' murmured Qenet, half to herself. Then she held out her hand to Josie and smiled again. 'It was a most kind and brave thing that you did for me. I see you are full of grace and giving. And you, too' – she turned to Ben, and gently touched his arm – 'you are knowing and careful; soon you will be sharp in courage and craft. I know; I have the *imbas forasnai* – the light of foresight. But I must ask you for more help yet. I have not come here for many hundreds of years. All will be strange to me. May I stay in your home tonight?' She opened her eyes wide in appeal. The bright torchlight finally dispelled any possibility of her being a normal human; for each of her irises contained three concentric rings of colour – brown, green and blue, the blue on the outside.

'Of course,' replied Josie impulsively. 'I'm sure mother and father won't mind. We told them about your message. They brought us here. They're waiting down on the road. Perhaps we'd all better go and tell them you've arrived.'

18

'O.K.' Qenet's familiarity with English was evidently growing rapidly. 'Ben, you lead please, with your light. Beware of demons and strangers, for this is Samain eve.'

Josie looked inquiringly but could detect no hint of irony in her expression. Ben seemed to take the request seriously. Searchlight in one hand, rounders bat in the other, he led them with an almost proprietorial air out of the barrow. Beyond the facade Qenet stopped and gazed upwards. 'Same old weather, at least,' she commented with a rueful smile. 'It was much better when they built the Stations. Samains were fine and warm; even Imbolcs were often mild.'

They made their way down the slope. Ben first, then Josie and Qenet. 'Do you live near here, Josie?' asked Qenet. 'My area of . . . ' – and she paused, seeking the right expression 'jurisdiction' – she wrinkled her nose – 'clumsy Latin word – goes over Downs and along my valley to Thames. I always tried to be a responsible goddess and they loved me here, until the Romans came. Smelly insensitive clods. Tried to integrate me with one of their own goddesses. Venus. Same with Sul at Bath over to the west. Sul Minerva they called her – made her look a right old bag.' She giggled and so did Josie. Ben merely snorted. 'I suppose Romans never came back, did they? That's why you speak a sort of Anglo-Saxon. Though you have some of their words.'

By now they were approaching the middle gate at the foot of the slope. Ben's light picked out two people waiting there. It was their parents. 'Any luck?' they heard their mother call.

'Yes, she's here, she's come.' Ben shouted and saw them both step back – presumably in amazement. Then Qenet slid past him. 'Hello, I'm *so* sorry to have caused all this trouble. So good of you and kind it was to allow Josie and Ben to meet me. I couldn't have arrived safely without them.'

Crumbs, thought Josie, she sounds just like a rich maiden aunt who's been met at the railway station. And indeed Qenet's manner seemed to have subtly changed. She looked the same (though it was too dark to see things very clearly) but her voice now sounded altogether more grown-up and authoritative. Before either of their parents could respond to her greeting, she had seized each of them by the hand. 'I'm terribly sorry to trouble you further,' she continued, 'but I would appreciate it if you could *possibly* spare me the time to explain the situation. I gather you're not familiar nowadays with inter-world transfer, so my arrival most likely seems wildly irrational to you. But, you see, I am in a bit of a fix at the moment.' She paused, in some way communicating a sense of honesty, maturity and sweet reasonableness to those around her.

19

The critical moment passed. Everyone seemed to relax. Josie and Ben's parents introduced themselves as they would to any stranger.

The group trudged back to the car across the damp and muddy field. Qenet ran forward. 'My river,' she exclaimed. 'It's here; after all these years. Has it still got my name?' Ben turned the beam of his torch on to the stream and Qenet stood precariously on the edge of the little bridge, gazing into the clear water below. She was obviously delighted. 'Has it still got my name?' she repeated.

Understanding dawned simultaneously on the others, but Ben got his answer out first. 'Yes,' he replied. 'Why on earth didn't I realise it before? Yes, it's still called Qenet. But it's spelt differently.'

'That doesn't matter,' said the goddess, examining the course of the stream as Ben's lamp followed it across the field. 'It wasn't spelt at all for the first 8,000 years. After the Ice, that is. But always has it been called Qenet.' She turned to the left and peered into the gloom. 'And my hill, is it still over there? Yes, I can just make it out.' She paused. 'Please forgive my excitement. I came here very often – it's only a month since I spent a week here – but that was 3,000 years ago. So far I've never been able to get nearer than 1,500 years to your sector of space-time. That's when the circles started to go bananas. Is that another exotic word? What I mean is that the synchroherence circuits began to malfunction. In the stone circles – the Series II Stations, that is. The trouble is that the Series I's – that's the long barrows like the one up there – had been decommissioned ages before. But luckily for me the shielding at West Kennett became ineffective about twenty-five years ago, so I was able to reactivate some of its receptor circuits – with your help, of course.' She beamed at them all, unaware of the incomprehensibility of what she had just said.

By now the party had reached the main road. Ben directed the beam of his light on to the orange Citroën. 'I suppose you've never seen a car before, Qenet,' he said, feeling rather silly. But Qenet didn't reply. She stood gazing entranced at the vehicle. Then she touched the paintwork and the windscreen and peered inside. 'So *that* is what your word "car" means,' she exclaimed, half to herself. 'A very prosaic and inadequate expression if I may say so. What a beauty. A real *siabur charput*. That means demon chariot in your language. A more fitting description altogether.' She grinned. 'If only Boudicca and Maeve had had some of these, they'd have zapped Paulinus and Cuchulainn for sure.' She sighed and looked up. Mrs Jameson opened the nearside front door. 'Hop in, we'll take you for a ride. Would you like a front seat?'

Qenet was torn between politeness and enthusiasm. She glanced inquiringly at Josie and Ben's father. 'Don't worry, I'll go in the back – it needs someone fairly tough to sit between these two hooligans to stop them brawling all the time,' he explained.

They showed Qenet how to fasten her seat-belt. The engine started and the headlight beams shone far into the darkness ahead. The car slowly rose as its hydropneumatic suspension cut in. 'Ooh, it feels alive,' commented Qenet, and then fell silent, gazing intently at passing vehicles, houses and villages as the car rushed home through the night.

Back home, in the warmth and light of the living-room, a slightly embarrassed pause ensued. It was Mr Jameson who re-solved it by asking outright if Qenet ate human food, or whether she had special needs – perhaps nectar and ambrosia? The goddess replied that it didn't matter. 'I'm not really carbon-based, you see,' she explained. 'More a stabilised energy form. Of course I radiate out infra-red heat like you do – so any high calorific fuel will do fine. It's a bit late in the season for nectar – honey will do nicely, if you've got any. Or alcohol. Or if necessary I can absorb energy direct from the atmosphere. Feel carefully.' And with that cryptic instruction she sat in a chair and closed her eyes. Almost at once the others understood what she meant. The heat drained from the room. Their breath became visible in the refrigerator-like air. Qenet opened her eyes again and the temperature began to rise immediately. Soon it was normal.

By eight o'clock that evening the main room of the Jamesons' house presented – at least gastronomically – an appearance of unusual variety. Ben and Josie were munching their way through large platefuls of egg, chips and baked beans. Ben had added some sardines to his meal and Josie some pickled gherkins and olives. Their parents were stoically eating salads. Qenet, still of course in her green-and-gold dress (*haute couture* by any standard and really more fitted to a formal evening out than to a nosh-up at home, felt Josie) was sampling the contents of seven identical glass bowls in front of her. From left to right they contained honey, Scotch whisky, condensed milk, blackcurrant jam, gin, golden syrup and *crème-de-menthe*. Two half-empty bottles of Ben's home brewed orange wine also stood on the table. It was quite a cheerful party. Qenet, between spoonfuls, had been asking a series of surprisingly detailed questions about the electrical equipment of the house. Already she had investigated the washing-machine, dishwasher, cooker, television and hi-fi. Now she was engaged in discussion with Ben and his father about the output of the local power-station, the red warning lights on the chimney of which had been visible from time to time on their return journey.

'Two thousand megawatts, you reckon? A big one by your standards? Coal-fired, then steam-driven turbines? Sounds rather inefficient. What do they do with all the steam afterwards? Throw it away?' She looked inquiringly at them and cautiously took a spoonful of *crème-de-menthe*. 'Wow, this is *lovely*. Goes with my dress too,' she added inconsequentially. 'I think I'll settle for this stuff.'

She paused, took a deep breath, and regarded her hosts with a rather diffident half-smile. 'I suppose I owe you an explanation. Here I come out of the mists of space-time, inveigle you into triggering the Transfer Station and bringing me here in your demon chariot and then ask you all these prying questions. You'll find my story difficult to understand, for you seem to be living in a non-symbiotic age. Even only 2,000 years ago they knew about symbiosis. Now it's all forgotten. Symbiosis means close co operation of different life forms for the benefit of all. Goddesses like me and Sul and Boan, humans like you, and the elves. *Are* there any elves in this sector, by the way?' she queried.

Josie explained about the various categories of non-human fairies – at least those that she could remember from her Brownie days – and their supposed place in the nature of things.

This didn't please Qenet. 'Your *sidhe* are no more than timorous sprites. No real clout. Elves aren't like that at all. They're a clever lot, cunning and subtle. Brilliant at mechanics and electronics. That's why we goddesses had a symbiotic relationship with them. People like me are really all energy. *Real* energy, that is, not your megawatts and megatons, but power to control the weather; power to cause earthquakes and volcanoes.'

She was getting quite worked up. Her eyes were wide open, their triple irises prominent. Her face and even her voice seemed once more to have taken on a more mature and authoritative expression. Ben felt his scalp tingling and his hair rising. 'Static,' he thought to himself. 'She's just like a walking Wimshurst machine. He unobtrusively brought his left index finger within an inch or two of one of the radiators, and was rewarded by a sharp jolting shock as he earthed himself. There was a smell of ionised air. Qenet stopped, looked surprised, and then smiled contritely. 'Sorry, I was getting carried away. Actually, I can only manage local weather by myself. For real tornadoes and cataclysms several of us would have to join forces. But I can control the regional climate quite well. That's why I was so well thought of around here during the New Stone Age. Corn isn't indigenous to this part of the world

22

at all, you know – it comes from the lands around the eastern Mediterranean – so the first farmers needed quite a lot of help. Not all the time, of course, but a good downpour occasionally and clear weather at harvest. And the ice had to be cleared away before we could even start to re-occupy the Downs around here.'

Ben interrupted, politely he hoped, for Qenet was emerging as a rather awe-inspiring person. 'Excuse my asking, but where do you get all this energy from? I mean, even to control weather locally must need a dreadful lot of power. Gigawatts and terawatts. And if you're talking about pushing back the ice-age glaciers, well . . .'

'From the sun, mostly,' explained the goddess in a matter-of-fact way. 'But anything'll do: volcanic heat, background radiation – not that there's much of *that* left nowadays – all the naturally formed atomic reactors packed up hundreds of millions of years ago, at least in this part of the universe. But there's plenty of fusion-energy in sunlight. I just mop it up and hold it. I bet you humans can't do that, can you? Your power-stations can churn out energy, but you can't store it. My guess is that all you can use are peripheral chemical and electrostatic effects – lead acid accumulators, sodium sulphur ones perhaps, and capacitors. Weedy, low-output toys, all of them. Not my league at all. That's what symbiosis is all about. I have the power, you humans need it to make life a little less difficult, and the elves are hot stuff on power conversion technology. Earth's always been a pretty lousy place to live in, you know. Always too hot or too cold. If you'd been around here 15,000 years ago you would know what I mean; howling blizzards and ice-sheets all the way to the North Pole. We put that right for you. Then once you humans developed metallurgy you all decided you could get along very nicely by yourselves, thank you. Well, perhaps you can for the present,' she conceded. 'But you just wait until you need *real* power again. When the deserts begin to spread, or the Ice starts crunching south. Or when you want to develop interstellar drive – then you'll all start pleading for help again. And next time you might not get it.'

There was a pause. 'I thought symbiosis was supposed to be a two-way relationship,' ventured Josie. 'At least that's what they teach us in Bilge. You know, like flowers providing bees with nectar and bees pollinating them. Each partner helps the other. What did humans do for you in return for the fine weather and all that?'

'Emotional drive and energy,' answered Qenet. 'After all, if you're mortal you have to be quick-witted and dynamic to survive. Goddesses and elves don't have to worry about that, so we tend to be a bit lazy. And you possess plenty of affection and devotion – we collect emotional energy as well as the crude sort. Crude energy gives one a sense of power, but it's a bit *impersonal*, if you know what I mean. Like facts and figures. Emotional energy gives one a warm feeling. Not that I've been getting much from this particular sector of space-time lately.' She looked around disapprovingly.

'So, you see, goddesses have power – but can only use it in rather unsubtle, if spectacular, ways; humans are very good at concepts – especially emotional ones – and at basic problem solving. But only the elves have ever been able to work out space-time interphasing. It seems to come naturally to them. They're always commuting between past and present and dodging between one world and another – as long as we provide the power, of course. Otherwise they're pretty unidimensional. And they need men to build their Transfer Stations – like the long barrow and the big stone circles at Avebury. Some of the later models – the Pi 3 series – are fabulous; they went in for miniaturisation, you know. So unless the elves design and maintain the transfer interface circuits, I'm pretty well stuck. Without power, they're pretty immobile too. And without either of us, humans just have to muddle along by themselves. I only managed to get through by myself because I've picked up some of the basic rudiments of transfer mechanics over the centuries. But I needed your help to receive my message and activate the Transfer Station. The energy gradient was in my favour too. Whether I'll be able to get back to the Otherworld without some elvish assistance is another thing altogether. That old Station felt pretty shaky to me – probably blew its circuits as I came through. Wouldn't like to try it again. I might become frozen in interdimensional stasis.' For a moment or two Qenet appeared definitely nervous.

'So what you really want to do as soon as possible', concluded Mrs Jameson, 'is to recruit an elf or two and a few humans to repair your Transfer Station. And have a look round, of course, to see what's going on nowadays. It looks as though you two' – she surveyed her children – 'are going to have a busy half-term.'

And on that note Qenet's first day in the twentieth century came to an end.

DAY THREE

It was fairly easy to work out a plan of campaign for the next day. Naturally enough, Qenet was anxious to take her first look in 1,500 years at what she referred to as her area of jurisdiction. Her interest centred on the Avebury circles, the long barrow itself and their associated monuments – Silbury Hill, the Kennet Avenue and the Sanctuary.

Still clad in her green-and-gold dress (it showed no signs of wear) and with her long hair braided in a complicated arrangement of plaits, she insisted that Josie and Ben should accompany her – not that they needed any persuasion. Paradoxically enough, the first problem was transport. For a being that could dodge in and out of space-time sectors with unconcern and ease, Qenet had to admit to severe limitations to her mobility on earth.

'It's the Statute,' she explained patiently at breakfast, sipping *crème-de-menthe* from a coffee-cup. 'Of *course* I could zoom around if I wanted to. Anywhere. But while I'm in human mode I've got to behave like a human. Or at least more or less like one. You'll never understand symbiosis unless you get the Statute of Limitations straight in your minds. Think of what it would be like if we could swan around any old how in your world. Miracles all over the place. Monsoons over the Sahara, sunny spells in Manchester. Thunderbolts every five minutes. Boan queening it over Ireland, Sul throwing her weight around in the West Country. Elves building monstrous Transfer Stations all over the place. Humans would degenerate into a lot of pampered serfs. And not all that pampered, either, in some places,' she added as an afterthought. 'Some of my lot can act quite bitchy. Elves can be pretty wild and wicked at times, too. So the Statute is quite specific. Limited intervention as far as immortals are concerned. Otherwise life here would end up as a succession of Trojan-type wars. And look at the mess *that* was. Aphrodite was most unethical to stir things up the way she did. Anyway,' she concluded, 'while I'm here I've got to act more or less like an ordinary human. No crash, bang, pow, from yours truly. So I'd be terribly grateful if I could use your lovely orange demon chariot. I'm sure I could learn to drive it quickly.'

And she did, too. Half an hour later, as their parents (looking rather dazed, but undeniably impressed) returned with Qenet from the latter's one and only driving lesson, Josie and Ben realised that the goddess had got her way. Ben, with recent memories of the long grind of lessons and practice runs which had preceded his own driving test, felt a twinge of envy. To Josie, however, Qenet's achievement seemed unremarkable. If the goddess could emerge through a solid rock wall and learn to speak fluent modern English within ten minutes it was hardly likely, she reckoned, that the mechanical complexities of driving would give her much trouble. Vaguely she wondered whether Qenet's style of driving would reflect the engaging raciness of her speech. She was not to be disappointed.

Suitably kitted out with anoraks, wellingtons, food and drink ('they'll charge the earth if you buy it'), the two of them climbed into the car. Qenet was already in the driver's seat; all *she* was taking, apparently, was the bottle of *crème-de-menthe* which appeared by common consent to have been assigned to her.

The car moved off. Ben, sitting in the back, again felt a slight sense of resentment as it accelerated, moving impeccably through the gears. Co-ordination of clutch and accelerator was a skill which had for a long time eluded him. He watched from behind as Qenet changed into top. Her crimson slipper depressed the clutch pedal, hesitated for a second and then released it. Just in front of him the gear lever, apparently of its own volition, slipped out of third and snicked into fourth. Was it magic, he wondered, or telekinesis? Perhaps the two were the same, he concluded. Maybe it depended upon one's viewpoint.

Soon they had gone through Swindon. Qenet was driving in an intent and absorbed way. She seemed to be gauging the performance of the car. Ascending Wroughton Hill, however, they found their progress blocked by a growling, smelly and seemingly infinite car transporter. The road, curving to the left, narrowed. Visibility was limited to a few yards. Qenet frowned. 'Blow this for a lark,' she murmured, and gunned the engine. As if in response the gear lever flew into second and the car swung into the opposite lane. Bearing down the hill dead ahead was an enormous red petrol-tanker. Its driver, his eyes staring and his mouth opening and closing involuntarily, looked about ten yards away. Then they were past the transporter, banking into their own side and leaving the other traffic far behind. Even the normally lightning-like reflexes of the lorry driver had not been fast enough to hoot or flash them before they were out of sight. To the left a spectacular coomb lay about fifty feet below the road level. On the right the hillside fell away precipitously, revealing wide views of the upper Thames valley.

26

'Qenet,' croaked Josie in a strangled voice, 'please, please, never ever do that again. You'll give me a heart attack.'

Qenet merely smiled. 'Don't get your knickers in a twist, dearie. We had almost thirty feet to spare – more than a whole second to get back into our lane. Nothing to worry about – driving's a cinch when you're used to interdimensional synchroherence adjustments. That tanker driver seemed a bit shattered, didn't he? Weak nerves. But I'll take it a bit easier if that's what you *really* want.'

Taking it easy, as far as Qenet was concerned, seemed to mean driving at a steady seventy miles an hour when the road was clear and at about fifty when it wasn't. Soon Ben and Josie learned to cultivate a detached view of things as the Citroën drifted round high-hedged corners and squeezed between the lorries and buses which appeared and flashed past in disconcerting proximity to the car.

Josie nudged Qenet. 'Careful, we're about there,' she warned. The massive stones of the Avebury circle appeared. Qenet frowned again. 'There shouldn't be a road through here,' she muttered as she steered the car through a ninety-degree bend to the right, turned off down the village street and shot into the car park. 'And what are all these houses doing inside my circle?'

She switched the engine off and looked around. She did not seem to like what she saw. Scowling, she stepped out of the car. 'The best preserved part's just down the street, off to the right,' explained Josie, hoping to mollify her, and, without waiting for a reply, she led the way to the north-west segment. Initially it seemed as though her efforts to cheer her companion up would be successful. The low autumn sun shone across the great circle, illuminating the stones and accentuating the gold in the green contours of the ditch and the tall bank beyond it. Qenet examined each stone in turn and began to relax a little. She even danced a few steps in evident delight around a two-seated sarsen not far from the mid-point of the arc. But once they had passed the Swindon Stone, crossed the road, and climbed up the rampart of the north-eastern quadrant, her black mood returned. For it was from here, along the eastern half of the main circle, that virtually all the stones had been removed. Even worse, apparently, was the ruin that had been inflicted upon the inner circles. The goddess stalked along the elevated path; Josie and Ben, feeling rather superfluous, trailed behind. Reaching the southern entrance to the circle, Qenet paused briefly to survey the towering Devil's Chair. Next, heedless of a herd of wary-looking cows, she walked across the grass to the remains of the more southerly of the minor circles. Hands on hips,

27

she stood behind the cement marker on the site of the obelisk and surveyed the Z stone alignment.

'Nothing but shame and shambles do I see around me on this dark day,' she declaimed to no one in particular. 'This isn't a circle, it's a wasteland. They make a desert, and call it an ancient monument. No wonder I couldn't get through. If only modern people could imagine the effort and time that went into making the circles here! They were the best in the whole wide world. Now look at them. Ruins, ruins!' She was almost crying. Impulsively she picked up a large flint from the ground and hurled it at the cement pillar. It bounced off with a thud.

'Oi!' shouted someone, and all three turned round to see a green-uniformed official striding round the corner of the nearest building. 'You can't do that. This is the property of the Ministry of Ancient Monuments. We don't put up with vandals here.' The man advanced right up to them. He was very cross. With sinking hearts Josie and Ben recognised him. On their last visit to Avebury they had watched with detached amusement as he harangued a mild-looking teacher who had arrived at the village car park with a party of junior school children in a minibus. 'Coaches in the Beckhampton Road field,' he had insisted. 'Get out or I'll report you to the police for illegal parking.' Now he stood self-importantly in front of Qenet and launched himself into a tirade about the misdemeanours of visitors – especially those of the younger generation. Then his jaundiced eye fell upon the goddess's long dress and her rather folksy hair-do. 'Hippies like you shouldn't be allowed in here,' he shouted. 'Layabouts and bloody kids, all of you. Ought to be put in labour camps. This whole place ought to be fenced off like Stonehenge is.' He was quite beside himself in anger and took a step towards Qenet, hoping perhaps to intimidate her.

To Ben his action seemed almost sacrilegious. 'Leave her alone, you old fool. You don't know who she is,' he shouted. Josie glanced at Qenet and saw at once that no human intervention was necessary. Qenet could look after herself. She stood quite still. She didn't even appear affronted or enraged. Just impassive. But her appearance was changing in a subtle, out-of-focus way. Her shiny hair seemed to become spiky and tangled, her face older and harsh; hag-like almost. Simultaneously the air temperature fell and the sunlight lost its power. The stones and houses around them took on a misty, insubstantial aspect. The four of them seemed all at once to be alone in a cold, hostile half-light. The attendant stuttered into silence and stopped uncertainly about a yard and a half in front of the goddess. Qenet began to speak, malevolently. 'Havoc on your thrice-damned head,' she hissed. 'No one, no one speaks to me like that. This is *my* place. Mine. Understand? Not your hollow neglectful Ministry's. You have destroyed my circles. Now with harsh screams and cruel heart you order me hence. One more word, *muc*, and I'll bring your guts down round your feet. I'll spike your head on the railings.'

Her left hand shot out, making what looked like a lateral karate chop at the horror-struck official. He screamed and staggered back as, for an instant, a blue flash flew between Qenet's fingers and his head.

Normality returned. The light and warmth of the sun flooded back; the mistiness vanished, revealing half a dozen curious onlookers. Qenet hadn't moved, but she had resumed her original young and pretty appearance. The man lay where he had fallen: he was alive and indeed still conscious. But his peaked hat had been sheared through between band and crown. The peak and a circle of material remained in place on his head, open at the top and revealing a neatly cut bare patch where the hair had been.

Qenet addressed him more in reproof than in anger. 'Remember this lesson, human. Never forget me, or that this is my place. And never speak to me, or of me, like that again. For there will be no second warning. Now beat it. Shove off. Go.' The attendant, clutching the detached part of his hat, got up. His eyes never left Qenet. He bowed awkwardly and backed away. The goddess ignored him, glanced at the knot of spectators, and turned to her companions. 'Thanks for offering to help,' she said. 'But I thought a direct lesson was called for. That stroke of precision is impressive, don't you think? One of my party tricks. It used to be a standard feature of sword training in the Bronze and Iron Ages. First a verbal warning to your foe. Next a quick slash at his shoulder-straps so that his clothes fell down.' She gave a sly smile, 'Then a stroke of precision to shave his head and finally the double cutting blow. Down the middle from skull to thigh and across the waist. Messy, but impressive. Four neat fillets of enemy warrior.'

Neither of the others could think of anything to say in reply to that, so the three of them resumed their perambulation of the circle. The south-west arc seemed in reasonable condition but most of the rampart, ditch and stones were fenced off. This, according to the notices, was to prevent soil erosion.

Back in the car park Josie tried to make the best out of what she knew to be a bad job. 'The western half of the outer circle's not too ruined, is it?' she began brightly. But Qenet was not to be comforted. 'That's the same as saying a punctured tyre's only got a small hole in it. The circle's had it.' She shrugged her shoulders. 'What's this Ministry thing that's supposed to look after the site?

They've not done much to restore it, have they? Cows all over the place, a main road slap through the middle of it and half the western part fenced off. It strikes me they *want* to keep it out of commission.'

Without further comment she started the car. Ben noted with admiration that this time she didn't even bother to turn the ignition key. They took the road to Beckhampton, turned left at the roundabout there and drove into the lay-by at the foot of Silbury. Leaving the car, they began to climb the hill. Qenet's eyes fell upon the fence that surrounded it and her brow darkened. 'Hell and damnation,' she exclaimed bitterly as she read the notice. 'Erosion,' they say again. 'This hill's been here for nearly 5,000 years and people have been climbing it all the time. Now this Ministry or whatever has the damned cheek to say it's going to fall down if we go up it.' She glared maliciously at the chestnut palings: five of them burst into flame, burned brightly for about half a minute and then collapsed in ashes. The wire holding them together became incandescent and disintegrated in a shower of sparks. 'Now we'll have lunch at the top,' she announced with an air of satisfaction. They returned to the car, collected their food and drink and charged light-heartedly to the summit of Silbury Hill.

Sitting on the flat space at the top and occasionally sipping *crème-de-menthe* while the other two ate ham sandwiches, Qenet seemed inclined to take a philosophical view of the dilapidated state of the Avebury monument. Perhaps her change of mood was connected with the reassuring solidity of Silbury itself and the sight of the long barrow's silhouette upon the south-eastern skyline. Anyway, she was prepared to concede that the twentieth century had a few good points: 'This green stuff's a great improvement on the beer they used to brew in the Iron Age. They had to drink it through their moustaches to strain the muck out. And that demon chariot of yours really turns me on.' She lay on her back and gazed thoughtfully at the contrails of a couple of high-flying Phantoms. 'I wouldn't mind a go in one of those. It would make Hecate and her noisy gang look a bit on the obsolescent side. You know,' she added by way of explanation, 'the Furies.'

The vision of Qenet howling through the sky in white overalls and a bone-dome was an attractive one, thought Ben. In fact, most aspects of her diverse character were. The other girls of his limited circle of acquaintance seemed rather anaemic in comparison. She wouldn't half cause a sensation at the local disco. For a few moments he was lost in thought, and only came to when Josie, with evident hesitation, asked a question that had been on her mind ever since the incident at Avebury. 'Qenet, when you blasted that poor twit over there in the circle, well, you seemed to sort of change. You looked a different person; deadly fierce. Or was it my imagination?'

Qenet gave her a sharp glance. 'Oh my goodness,' thought Josie, 'I've gone and offended her.' Then the goddess's face cleared and she smiled condescendingly. 'I may be a bit naive about the state of affairs in this sector of space-time, but you're absolutely pig-ignorant yourselves about the past – if you'll forgive my saying so. All half-decent goddesses in this part of the world are triune. Three-way schizophrenics, I guess you could call us. Even the Romans and Greeks knew about *that*. Ever heard of Artemis, Selene and Hecate? Same goddess, different personalities. When she was on earth Artemis was an outdoor-girl type – quite sexy in an athletic kind of way. As a moon goddess she was called Selene – all mysterious and seductive. But when she visited the underworld she was known as Hecate – and a real terror she could be, take my word for it. I've got three modes too. I usually keep to the helpless-maiden one' – she winked at Josie – 'it helps no end with most humans, especially men. But I can turn to the second mode if I like – that's the serious, mature lady; it's useful if I want to impress anyone important – like your parents for example. And when I really want to blow my top I go automatically into Mode 3, that's what you saw down in Avebury. Scares the living daylights out of people,' she concluded in a matter-of-fact way.

Ben broke in. 'That stroke of precision. I wanted to ask you about that. Did the Iron Age warriors really shave their enemies' hair like that? And then cut them in four like you said?'

'Only the heroes and heroines; tricks of the trade really. They called them "feats" and had to practise for years to get them right. The stroke of precision was one of them; the salmon-leap was another – that's jumping up on to your enemy's shield so you can hack his head off. I'll show you yet another if you like – the stunning shot. Watch.'

She selected a stone from the ground by her hand, stood up and hurled it at a flight of lapwings as it flew overhead. One of them stopped flapping and spiralled gracefully down. Gently Qenet caught it and showed it to the others. 'No harm done,' she explained, and stroked the reviving bird. 'Easy when you know how.' She tossed the lapwing into the air. It flew without any apparent difficulty, gained height and vanished into the distance.

Together they wandered over to the eastern side of the hilltop. 'There's your river,' said Ben, pointing to the line of trees that marked the course of the Kennet. Qenet followed the direction of his arm. 'Now *that's* changed,' she exclaimed. 'The spring used to

31

rise right under here. Very impressive and charming it looked, with the water gushing out of the mound. Symbolic, you know. Now the river's retreated towards Avebury. I suppose the water table's risen. Pity. Still I expect your rotten Ministry would have diverted it anyway. Probably into the local sewage works. Come on, let's go and inspect the barrow. The circle's finished as a Transfer Station and if the barrow's on the blink too, I've got problems. I don't fancy being stuck in this tatty backyard of space-time longer than I have to be.'

She gave Ben a playful shove down the slope and then ankle-tapped him. Ben gave his standard impersonation of a shot soldier and snatched one of her shoes as he fell. Qenet overbalanced, grabbed Josie and all three of them careered down the side of the hill, directing their course through the incinerated section of the fence. Then they picked themselves up and ran along the road to the signposted footpath which led to the barrow.

Ten minutes later they had reached the enclosure at the top of the rise. Two men were working there. They were hammering in stakes around the entrance. 'What's going on here?' Ben called out. The nearer of the labourers put his heavy mallet down and came over, grinning affably. Then his eyes fell on Qenet and he gave a wolf-whistle. 'What's up?' he inquired. 'Anything I can do for you, love?'

'I said "what's going on?" ' repeated Ben. 'We were all here yesterday and there was no sign of a barrier. Just a pile of materials.' The man looked at him. 'O.K., squire, keep your hair on,' he replied. 'We've got to close this site up, Ministry orders. Some professor geezer wants to do archaeological experiments here or something. That's so, isn't it, Charlie?' He turned for confirmation to his companion. The latter nodded. 'Yes, that's it. They're closing up the site over at the Sanctuary, too. See?' He pointed across the shallow valley to Overton Hill where a couple of Range Rovers and a lorry could be discerned in the lay-by opposite a transport café. Several figures could be made out and a certain amount of equipment seemed to have been dumped on the site.

An exclamation from Qenet caused them to turn round. The goddess's eyes were fixed on the centre stone of the barrow's facade; her face was pale and she swayed from side to side as if she were about to collapse. Josie and Ben each grabbed one of her arms while one of the men hastily kicked a roll of wire out of the way as they half carried her to one of the lowest stones and sat her on it. 'What's the matter, love?' asked Charlie, as he pushed her head down to her knees. 'Thanks, I'm better now,' said Qenet's muffled voice after a minute or so, and she sat up. 'Sorry, it must be jet lag.

I've just come a long way.' She shook her head and smiled faintly. She struggled to her feet and walked over to the great centre stone. 'When did this happen?' she asked, pointing to a shallow depression in the middle of its outward-facing surface. 'It wasn't here yesterday, was it?'

Ben and Josie shrugged; they couldn't remember. The silence was broken by Charlie: 'No, the old prof did it this morning, didn't he? He sent one of his sidekicks up here to tell us to get out of the way for quarter of an hour. Then he lined up his surveying gubbins on the stone. You know, one of those death-ray things . . .' 'Lasers,' interjected Ben. The man nodded. 'That's it, a laser. He's got a mobile generator for it in the lorry over there. Says it's incredibly accurate for measuring distances . . .' His voice tailed off uncertainly.

'You don't need a high-power laser for surveying work,' said Ben, puzzled. 'It must have a terrific punch to bash a dent into that rock. I thought lasers like that were classified as secret weapons – they're thinking of using them to burn out enemy missiles. A low-powered gas laser such as the one we have at school is all that's needed for surveying.' He glanced nervously towards Overton Hill. 'Perhaps we'd better all get out of the way. Those things will pulverise steel plate.'

'Ben, what's a laser?' asked Qenet. She looked excited and the triple irises of her eyes were showing up vividly. 'I haven't got a clear picture in my mind. Tell me, please.'

'Acronym', replied Ben in his best lecture-theatre voice, 'for Light Amplification by Stimulated Emission of Radiation. It pumps up energy and releases it in incredibly short pulses of coherent light. Each pulse can carry as much power as hundreds of generating stations. Wham! Sometimes described as a brilliant invention seeking a real use.'

'Thanks,' said Qenet and turned to Charlie and his companion. 'This professor, what does he look like, and what's his name?'

'Short-arsed little so-and-so,' answered Charlie. 'Five foot fourish, I guess. Hairy beard and fuzzy moustache. Talks to you as if you were dirt. But they say he's a big noise down at Salisbury University. Does archaeology there. Works with the Ministry a lot. A real buddy of old Dudley Spatchcock's – he's the Permanent Secretary. He's got a funny name – Snood? Snide?'

'Snid,' said Qenet. 'That's it, glamour puss,' confirmed the more flirtatious of the two workmen. 'Know him?' Qenet gave him a hard look. 'Longer than you could guess, buster. Mind if we take a quick look inside the barrow?'

Once they were in the chamber she beckoned Josie and Ben to

come close. 'Snid!' She almost spat the word out. 'Snid. Of course, it would have to be. Well, Ben, it seems as though a real use has been found for the lasers after all. That professor they were talking about – he's no more human than I am. Snid the Fink they call him. An elf, officially, though if you ask me he's more of a goblin. Ambition, vice and buffoonery in equal proportions. That king-sized laser he's got over there, sure as sure he's trying to use it as a synchroherence interface stabiliser. Heaven alone knows what he'll end up by doing. Last time he tried mucking around with synchromechanics he dumped himself in the middle of the Ice Age by mistake. I wish he'd stayed there along with the woolly mammoths.' She stamped her foot. 'And what the hell does he mean by posing as a human? It's not allowed – at least not on a professional or executive basis. Immortals can only do it in an observer capacity. Trust a misbegotten pestering demon like him to team up with your precious Ministry, too. No wonder they've shut off Stonehenge, Silbury, Avebury and now the Sanctuary and the long barrow here. He's probably planning a takeover bid for all the main Transfer Stations.'

Another thought struck her. 'And what's he hoping to use for power?' she snapped. 'Not me, or any other goddess. None of the others would *dare* supply the energy to operate one of my stations. No, he'll have to be using some bodged-up man-made power source. That mobile generator thing he's got over at the Sanctuary is bound to be utterly inadequate. Snid must have something more effective up his sleeve. Anyway, it's high time he had his knuckles rapped, and his Ministry collaborators, too. If they can break rules, so can I – well, a bit, anyway.'

Qenet composed herself into statuesque immobility, looking as she did when she first appeared on the previous day. She remained still for perhaps a minute and her eyes were flickering open when Charlie came into view at the entrance to the tomb. 'Quick, come and have a look,' he shouted. 'They've got trouble over at the Sanctuary. Generator lorry's blown up, or something.'

They charged outside. The largest of the three vehicles parked on Overton Hill was ablaze. Already dense smoke was drifting across the main road, while several small figures could be seen running away from it. 'Well, they had no right to go messing about with my Transfer Station,' Qenet said – a little defensively, maybe. 'And I think it's high time we went and sorted friend Snid out.'

Waving cheerily to the workmen, she led the way down the slope. As they followed the now familiar path she explained how the Station had worked in the New Stone Age, 5,000 years before.

'It was a fairly unsophisticated Series I model – but as tough as old boots. The trigger coding for interdimensional transfer was transmitted along a beam from a round house at the top of Overton Hill. The house itself was pretty well perfectly aligned with the passage into the barrow and was positioned at the same altitude. The procedure was quite simple; you just waited in one of the side chambers out of the way of the beam until the interface stabilised and then you crossed the barrier. It worked well enough for hundreds of years. Then, soon after metal technology had been discovered, they established that stone circles could accept far higher synchroherence loadings. First they built them round a few of the Series I stations – Boan's place at New Grange was a case in point – and then they gave up using the chambered barrows altogether. They ritually blocked them up and sealed them off. From then on they just used circles – Series II Stations, that is. Avebury was the biggest. Later on they developed the Pi 3 circles. They were flattened circles of stones with a circumference/diameter ratio of 3, as opposed to the usual 3·1416. There were never many of them and they were much smaller, but they really were fantastic. A.A.A. category. Anything, Anywhere, Anywhen. One of the elves assigned here – Mar Ten, his name is – did a lot of research and development work on the new units at the Durrington experimental establishment. I'll never forget the calibration trials at my own first Pi 3 circle about a mile from here over at Langdene. There was I, pumping out 5 terawatts and almost blowing my gaskets while Mar Ten stood there biting his nails and trying not to look worried as the stones began to get red hot. And naturally there was a great mob of humans all waiting to see the show – the place is a natural amphitheatre, you know. Anyway, nothing happened for seven and a half minutes and then Bingo! Zonk! I thought we'd fused the interlock circuits. But it was only the materialisation shock wave caused by a hulking great tyrannosaur. It hardly fitted into the circle. Everyone stampeded out of the way. It certainly made an impression – probably they still have a legend about it in the villages around here! Mar Ten almost died laughing – all elves have a juvenile sense of humour, you know. Luckily we managed to get it back to the Cretaceous Age before it could lumber out of the circle and do any damage. If anything, Langdene was better even than Avebury for time-transfer,' she explained reflectively. 'Though nothing could touch the Avebury complex for inter- and intra-dimensional travel, especially when the circles at Brodgar in the Orkneys and Lios in Ireland were linked in.'

By now they had reached the car. Just as they were pulling out of the lay-by a police motorcyclist appeared round the bend from the direction of Overton Hill and Marlborough. His lights were flashing and he brought his motorbike across the road into the eastbound lane ahead of them. He stopped, dismounted and held up his arm. Qenet brought the car to a stop beside him. She lowered the window and smiled winningly. The policeman blinked, blushed and cleared his throat. 'Sorry, Miss,' he began, 'there's been an explosion up the hill ahead. A mobile generator's blown up and the oil's caught fire and spread all over the road. If you want to go to Marlborough you'll have to take the back way through East Kennett and Lockeridge. They've got a couple of fire appliances but they can't seem to stop the flames. Foam hasn't worked so they're running hoses down to the river. It looks a cross between the fifth of November and a volcanic eruption. No one can get within twenty yards.'

Qenet pouted. 'Oh dear, I *so* wanted to see Professor Snid. He's in charge there, you know. Was he hurt in the explosion?'

The policeman shrugged. 'He's the boss there, all right. No, he wasn't hurt. But he looked scared to death when I saw him a few minutes ago. Kept muttering about sabotage and saying it was the fault of the river – you know, the Kennet. They wanted to take him to hospital for shock but he refused to go. Shot off to Devizes museum in a hurry just before I came away. He's in a green Range Rover. If you step on it you might just catch him up. Would you like me to escort you? If it's urgent, I mean.' He blushed again and shifted his feet uncomfortably.

Qenet gave him a wide-eyed smile. Ben could have kicked her and even Josie thought that she was rather overdoing it. 'Thanks, officer,' she murmured. 'That would really be most helpful.' She restarted the engine and eased the car up behind the motorcycle.

The ride to Devizes was more hair-raising, if possible, than the journey to Avebury. Their escort seemed to be piling on the speed, possibly to impress Qenet. The goddess herself, travelling through country that had been familiar to her 1,500 years previously (but not since then), persisted in looking all over the place in her attempts to relocate ancient landmarks. 'Where's my circle?' she shouted as they accelerated to seventy-five along the narrow lane from East Kennett past Langdene Bottom. 'Vandalised, I suppose. What's happened to the Wansdyke?' she asked a few minutes later as they shot through the gap made in it for the road. 'Look,' she cried as they hurtled along the straight towards Alton Hill. 'The old camp's still there and so is Adam's Grave.' She pointed and craned her head from side to side as the two vehicles began their power-dive into the Vale of Pewsey, dizzy vistas of which opened up to their left as they careered down the twisting road. A mile or so further on all four wheels of the car left the road as they bounced over a humpbacked bridge at Honey Street. A confused succession of twisting lanes and centrifugal corners soon led them into Devizes. Qenet swung the car expertly into the small parking space behind the museum. She fluttered her long, dark lashes at the policeman (whose admiration of her looks was now doubtless augmented by an appreciation of her driving capabilities), tactfully declined his offer to take her to Silverstone the following Saturday, and, together with Josie and Ben, entered the museum.

A young lady wearing an arty-crafty purple dress with a black jet necklace and plastic arrowhead earrings was sitting at the reception desk. She looked inquiringly at them. Qenet poked Josie in the ribs with her elbow. 'Go on,' she whispered. 'You ask.'

'We're trying to find Professor Snid,' began Josie. 'The people over at the Sanctuary said he was coming here.'

The girl seemed puzzled. 'I thought he'd finished his work here,' she said. 'Let me check.' She rang an internal extension, spoke briefly and replaced the phone. 'Yes, I mean no, he's not here, I'm afraid. Is he a friend of yours?' They shook their heads in unison. Encouraged, the girl leaned forwards. 'To tell the truth, we don't like him much. He's kind of creepy. And his assistant is even worse. Mr Slugwam. What a name. *I* wouldn't care to go down into the storage cellars alone with either of them. And Snid slings his weight around so much. Do you know what he wanted to do? He told – not asked, mind you – the curator that he wanted to take the Fyfield and Upavon sun-discs away – for analysis and examination, he said. Just like that.' She looked at them, obviously expecting them to share in her condemnation of this enormity.

'Hmm,' said Qenet, 'I'm afraid we're all a bit vague about what you've got here. I haven't been around for some time.'

The girl glanced round to make sure no one else was listening. 'They're early Bronze Age gold and amber discs – about an inch in diameter. Gold round the outside, amber in the middle. Probably unique. No one knows what they were originally used for, but they were excavated from two of the best known Wessex round barrows. They're upstairs in the Stourhead Room if you want to have a look.'

Then her eyes fell upon the goddess's bracelets. 'Where on earth did you get those?' she stammered out. 'They're Celtic electrum torcs, aren't they?' Qenet slipped one off and handed it over. The girl examined it eagerly. 'This must be priceless,' she exclaimed. 'It's a miniature version of the Snettisham torc in the British Museum. Those curvilinear ends – insular Waldalgesheim style. I studied Celtic jewellery at university. Fabulous; fantastic.' She caught her breath and peered more closely. 'It's genuine electrum, isn't it? Gold-silver alloy, hand-drawn. I didn't know anyone could produce work like that nowadays. It's – it's not *original* is it? It couldn't be, not in this condition,' she concluded, regretfully handing the bracelet back. 'And your dress. Marvellously compatible, that lovely Celtic gold pattern. Where did you get it from? Annabelinda's?' She stopped, as though becoming aware of the one-sidedness of the conversation. 'Sorry, I was babbling on a bit. Look, nobody's around, so it won't matter if I come up and show you the discs.' She left her seat and led them through a couple of galleries and up a flight of stairs. At the top she turned left into a smallish room. She pointed to one of the display cases. 'Here you are. Those are the sun-discs that his lordship wanted to swipe. Lovely, aren't they? Would you like me to ask the curator if he'll come and let you have a closer view? I'm afraid I can't open the case myself; security is pretty tight here, you know.'

'Don't bother,' answered the goddess, squeezing her nose up against the glass to inspect the discs as closely as possible.

They all had a good look. Each sun-disc consisted of a small golden circle enclosing a reddish centre. The latter were quite opaque. 'Deactivated,' announced Qenet. 'They're the lenses and ringmounts from a standard Series I interface stabiliser. Terawatt capacity. No wonder Snid wanted to get his hot little hands on them . . .' She became aware that the others were watching her curiously. 'Yes, beautiful, isn't it,' she continued. 'Middle or Late Neolithic – say around 3000 BC?' 'No,' said the girl firmly, 'a good deal later – more like 1800 BC. Certainly post-Beaker period.'

'Nuts,' replied Qenet with authority. '1800 BC must be your *terminus ante quem*. In other words the discs were buried around 1800 BC.' The girl nodded. 'They were made much earlier, and handed over to the local chiefs when the Series I Transfer Stations were taken out of commission. That was about 2250 BC, if my memory serves me correctly. Then they were kept as sacred relics for about four or five hundred years. Eventually they were buried in Bronze Age round barrows along with their last owners.'

Qenet's manner discounted argument and the museum receptionist obviously didn't know what to make of what she had said, conflicting as it did with the accepted archaeological view. There was a rather awkward silence until Josie tactfully changed the subject by asking the price of the fancy tea-towels with Ancient Britons printed on them which she had seen at the desk. In a spirit of self-sacrifice she actually bought one. But the young lady looked at them very oddly as they left.

Outside and in the car Josie grabbed Qenet's bottle and took a quick swig. 'That's a bit better,' she said. 'Qenet, you really *must* remember that people aren't used to goddesses. They think you're a myth. And time travel exists only in science fiction as far as they're concerned. So do watch what you say, for goodness' sake – otherwise you'll end up in a padded cell.' She glanced nervously at Ben, but he was gazing out of the window, non-involvement written all over his face, so she plunged on. 'And another thing, don't you think you're asking for trouble, going round in a thin silk dress with those gold bracelets on? You'll get yourself mugged, or indecently assaulted, or something.'

Qenet didn't seem at all put out. 'Don't worry, old thing,' she replied in a soothing voice. 'Qenet can look after herself – remember the Ministry man at Avebury this morning? But I'll buy myself a brown woollen cardy if you think it'll make me a bit less conspicuous. Where's the nearest dress shop?' She got out and opened Josie's door. 'Come on, Missy Prissy. We won't be long, Ben. Seeya.'

It was becoming dark when they returned. Qenet was wearing a long cardigan of Jacob's sheep wool which effectively concealed the more exotic features of her original attire. She guided the car in and out of the homegoing traffic without any of the hair-raising manoeuvres which had so worried her passengers earlier on. They were back in time for tea, which they took sitting round the television and watching the Wombles ('fascinating – a genuine folk-tradition,' Qenet commented) and then the news. This included an item on the official opening of a reservoir in the north of England. The newsreader explained that the project had been carried through despite the opposition of the people living in two local villages, both of which were due to be submerged under the new artificial lake. A number of the buildings thus to be destroyed were listed as being of outstanding historical interest. The Ministry of Ancient Monuments, however, had overruled all objections and had indeed been represented at the ceremony by none other than Sir Dudley Spatchcock, its Permanent Secretary. The picture switched to the site, where a reporter stood at the edge of the rising water, a row of half-flooded dwellings behind him. 'But today's official junketings were rather spoiled', he was saying, 'by the sudden indisposition of Sir Dudley. At the reception after the ceremony he was taken ill and rushed to Newcastle General Infirmary. The doctors there have diagnosed an acute attack of theic allergy.' His solemn tone changed. 'In other words Sir Dudley has become sensitised to tea. Ha! Ha! A devastating blow for a civil servant! Latest reports state that the patient is bearing up and that his medical advisers have hopes of his being able to start

39

drinking small amounts of weak Keemun tea within a few weeks' time.'

The scene shifted back to the studio. The announcer was grinning all over her face. Then, realising she was on camera, she abruptly resumed her habitual aloof expression and continued with the remaining items.

The regional news was even more interesting. There was a long feature on the explosion on Overton Hill and the unaccountable violence of the fire which had followed. 'Professor Snid of Salisbury University was at the time conducting laser surveying experiments on the site. In recent years he has become one of the best known of Britain's younger generation of archaeologists. His discovery of the spectacular Wash Treasure – lost by King John in the early thirteenth century – followed by his well publicised work at the previously unknown Phoenician Bronze Age trading-post on Bryher in the Scilly Isles, has marked him out as one of the most brilliantly intuitive of our researchers into the past. After today's incident he was interviewed at Salisbury by our reporter.'

The picture switched to show a male figure, which, emerging from a building of unusual and austere design, walked towards the camera. It stopped in front of a notice which read 'Salisbury University Department of Archaeology. Experimental Laboratory', and the camera zoomed in.

Professor Snid appeared to be a fairly small man of about fifty. He was wearing cowboy-style boots, a cream-coloured safari suit and a mauve shirt with a green silk scarf. Not much of his face was visible, for he had longish hair, a thin beard, and a macho moustache. His eyes were almost invisible behind tinted, silver-rimmed spectacles. 'Cor, what a dude!' commented Josie in disgust. But Snid seemed affable enough. He explained to the interviewer that he had been engaged upon a preliminary survey of the elevations and distances between the Sanctuary and the neighbouring sites at West Kennett and Silbury Hill. These, he continued, might provide valuable data concerning the relationship of the prehistoric monuments and perhaps even give some clues as to why the sites themselves had been selected in the first place. He was beginning to get into his stride when the interviewer interrupted him. 'I'm sure all our viewers will find this fascinating,' he said, 'but could we have your explanation of today's incident? As you know, Professor, the area is supposed to be haunted by a huge dragon. Can your experiments have disturbed it? Certainly your equipment got all burned up! Or can there be a sort of curse on the once sacred places of our earliest ancestors?'

Snid's eyes glinted behind the spectacles. 'I'm a man of science,' he asserted. 'I've no time for superstitious nonsense. All my work is carried out with the full co-operation of the Ministry of Ancient Monuments and any interference with it' – he paused and gave a wintry smile – 'whether by human or supernatural agency, will be dealt with appropriately.' The picture faded as the interview came to an end.

'Supercilious old fool,' snorted Qenet, evidently nettled by Snid's warning, 'full of pride and haughtiness as ever. When he talks like that I hear red battle's distant roar.' She sighed. 'I suppose I'd better go down to Salisbury tomorrow and read the riot act to him. Or at least try to. If all he's trying to do is get out of this sector of space-time I'll be glad to help him – with my foot if necessary. But he'll get a real rocket if it's ever discovered that he's been ignoring the Statute by posing as a human and trying to operate a Transfer Station without permission.'

'Surely you're doing the same thing, aren't you?' protested Ben. 'You're pretending to be a human. And turning the old feminine charm on and off like Mata Hari.'

'I've never denied I was a goddess, nor stated that I was human,' replied Qenet loftily, 'and I never will, even if they do try to put me in a padded cell. And as for intersexual friendships with humans, who has ever said there's anything against *that*? Doesn't anyone read mythology nowadays?' And she turned back to watch the television.

DAY FOUR

The ride to Salisbury the next morning was an uneventful one. As it was Sunday there wasn't much traffic on the roads. Qenet drove the Citroën carefully over the Downs into the Vale of Pewsey and through Upavon. The fine autumn weather was continuing. Just as the road was leaving the Vale to follow the Avon into the valley which it had carved over the centuries through Salisbury Plain, Qenet brought the car to a halt by a clump of shrubby trees.

'That's hazel, isn't it?' she asked. 'I'm going to need a branch. Could you help me get one, please.' She jumped out followed by her rather mystified companions and selected a fairly straight length of wood. 'Now, my proud warrior,' she said challengingly to Ben, 'cut it here and here. Two blows of your crimson blade should suffice.' Of course, they didn't. But Ben's Opinel knife soon managed to hack off a length about two feet long. Qenet took the knife and began to strip the bark off. 'Going to beat Snid up?' inquired Josie, half seriously. 'We could have brought the rounders bat for that.' Qenet shook her head, 'No, hazel's a traditional sign of neutrality and negotiation. Snid will have to see me, whether he's at the university or at home, if I present him with this. And he'll have to behave himself, too.' She held the hazel wand at arm's length and gave it an experimental swish or two. This appeared to satisfy her, so they all piled into the car and started the last stage of the journey.

Rather to Ben's surprise, Qenet suggested that he should drive the rest of the way. She sat beside him, disapprovingly eyeing the haphazard and unlovely buildings that surrounded the military installations along the valley. At Durrington they drew over to the right hand side of the road and briefly examined the unprepossessing remains of Woodhenge, then they continued the journey through Amesbury, with its strange, frontier-town atmosphere. Three miles out of Salisbury the first signposts for the university began to appear and then, just past the conical hillfort of Old Sarum, they swung off to the right into the campus itself.

Salisbury University was a relatively recent foundation. The main buildings, put up to accommodate a College of Advanced Technology in the late 1950s, were beginning to look rather tatty round the edges. They were dominated, however, by the hangars of the Department of Aerospace Technology. The angular lay-out of the access roads underlined the aerodrome-like quality of the place. Ben was cautiously negotiating one of the frequent intersections when Qenet, without warning, yelled at him to stop. As though to emphasise the urgency of her order she clamped her foot down over his on the brake pedal. The car seemed to stand on its nose. Ben was hurled forward and his forehead almost banged on the windscreen. Gasping from the pressure of the seat belt he looked around, seeking the cause of the goddess's excitement. He soon spotted it. The road ahead was clear, but to the right, parked on permanent exhibition, was one of the prototype Concordes. Qenet was gazing at it with intense admiration. Before either Josie or Ben could stop her she had ducked out of the car, jumped over the low fence surrounding the aircraft and was peering up at the massive engine cowlings. For about a quarter of an hour she inspected the plane, firing questions about its operation and performance to an increasingly apprehensive Ben. There was something childlike about her absorption. The impending confrontation with Snid appeared forgotten and Ben found it hard to contain his impatience. 'She's behaving as though she had all the time in the world,' he muttered. 'Well, she *has*, hasn't she, you goon?' his sister responded tartly. 'Things must seem different when you're immortal. That's what she meant when she said that goddesses needed humans to jog them along. Go on, tell her to get a move on, or I will.'

Ben, not for the first time in the last few days, began to feel a bit henpecked. Josie and Qenet between them, he reflected gloomily, were rather too much of a good thing. They even looked alike, for today Josie was wearing a long floppy Indian cotton dress, which resembled Qenet's in style. And she had rearranged her hair too. He nerved himself to interrupt Qenet but he was saved from risking the goddess's displeasure by a blast on the horn from a minibus which had found its progress blocked by the empty Citroën. It was crammed with students who were waving genially and already making mildly suggestive remarks to both Qenet and Josie. The former waved back to her new admirers and returned to the car. Ben started the engine and drove past the cavernous buildings of the Aerospace Department towards the smaller but more imposing ones belonging to Archaeology.

The Department of Archaeology at Salisbury University was housed in two sections: the administration-tuition block and the experimental laboratory. They were identical in appearance and joined by a single-storey entrance hall. Their distinctive design was based closely upon that of the famous pylon gateway of the great Egyptian temple at Karnak. The main parts of the building

43

were each about thirty yards long and fifteen deep. They had two floors and the walls sloped inwards from the foundations up to the flat roofs. The surfaces were of black glass and even the windows were tinted. The site as a whole managed to convey an impression of grandeur and, to the visitors at least, one of quiet menace. The austerity of the architecture was offset only by twin circles of white ceramic displayed in the middle of each top storey. The right-hand one depicted in mosaic the university's coat of arms. The one on the left contained an unfamiliar device: a five-clawed starfish-shape in black, each finger rounded like a sickle and tipped with red. The same emblem was repeated on the doors of the three green Range Rovers parked outside the main entrance.

Ben slowed the orange Citroën and cruised past the forecourt. Then, at Qenet's whispered request, he accelerated and followed the service road as it circled back to the central car park.

'I thought we were going to case Snid's place,' complained Josie, but in reality she was quite glad to leave the Archaeology Department behind. It gave her the creeps. 'What's the matter, Qenet?'

'That sign,' half-muttered the goddess, 'I don't like the look of it. Not one little bit. I've seen it before, back in the late New Stone Age. It's the Claw of Krasnog. You wouldn't have heard of him. Third millenium BC, Battle Axe Culture of north Germany. Organised an army of uncouth thugs and carved out a tribal kingdom for himself. He was a psychopath if you ask me. Enjoyed killing people in all manner of nasty ways. Not a symbol you would expect to be adopted by a reputable twentieth-century academic.'

They left the car. The ominous appearance of the Archaeology buildings, coupled with Qenet's account of Krasnog, had taken the edge off what had promised to be an enjoyable and adventurous day. In a group they wandered back to Snid's headquarters. Just outside the forecourt they paused.

'I'm going in now,' announced Qenet, holding the hazel rod in her right hand. 'How about you two having a snoop around to see what you can find out about the laboratory. Don't let anyone see you if possible and don't go in unless the coast is clear. And if you do see anyone, get out quickly. Especially if he's carrying a stone battle-axe.' She wasn't joking.

As soon as Ben and Josie had disappeared round the back of the building, Qenet turned and walked across the forecourt, past the green Range Rovers and up the shallow steps which led into the entrance hall. The dark plate-glass doors swished open automatically as she approached and closed behind her, sealing her off in the twilight of the interior.

The foyer was warm and stylish. A lot of money had been spent on it. The floor was grey-carpeted, the walls of black marble and the ceiling of smoke-tinted glass behind which was concealed the source of the subdued lighting. At regular intervals along the inside walls were a number of floodlit niches, each containing an electrotype copy of one of the more spectacular archaeological finds of the last century or so: a golden helmet from Cotofanesti, the Mold pectoral, the Milston dagger, an elaborate Danish belt disc, a golden mask from Mycenae, and a statue of the demon Pazuzu from Babylonia. In the centre of the room, on a granite pedestal, stood a reproduction of the celebrated and beautiful head of the Egyptian queen Nefertiti. Qenet returned its blank gaze and marched straight to the reception desk situated directly behind it. A well groomed young lady in black surveyed her with cool neutrality. 'Was there something?' she asked. 'You bet there is, babyface,' replied Qenet unceremoniously. 'I wanted to see Snid. And quick.'

The girl sat quite still. The silver-varnished nails of one hand tapped lightly on the desk-top as she gave the goddess an appraising stare. Impressed by her visitor's air of confidence and elegant appearance she decided to play it cool; perhaps she was the Vice-Chancellor's latest girl-friend or even the daughter of a potential university sponsor. '*Professor* Snid', she enunciated, 'is not available today. Tomorrow morning' – she referred to a leather-bound diary – 'he will be visiting the causewayed camp at Abingdon and then the Rollright Stones in north Oxfordshire. For the rest of the week he will be supervising the laser survey at the Kennett sites.' She managed somehow to convey the impression that the country's economy would collapse should he in any way fail to carry out this schedule. 'If you would care to leave your name and reason for wanting an appointment,' she concluded, 'I'll refer your request to him.' She picked up a biro and looked inquiringly at Qenet, who smiled sweetly back at her. 'I don't think you quite understand,' she said. 'I want to see Snid and I want to see him now. Not after lunch, not tomorrow, not some time next week. And you're going to get off that neat little bottom of yours and go and tell him just that. Understand? If he finds out you've been trying to give me the brush-off he'll chop you up into little pieces. And if he doesn't, I will. So move it. Say an old friend's come to see him. Give him this.' She held out the hazel rod and tapped the girl lightly on the head with it. The girl's eyes flashed with suppressed anger as she gingerly took the wood. She bit her lip, then rose without a word and stalked out of the room. Qenet waited. The girl returned. She looked straight through the goddess. 'He'll see you now,' she said tonelessly. 'This way, please.'

She led the way along a softly carpeted corridor. At the end she

45

stopped, tapped a fumed-oak door and whispered. 'Your visitor's here, Professor' into an intercom mounted in the wall. She marched back the way she had come without any further glance at Qenet. The latter, the ghost of a smile on her lips, watched her vanish into the gloom.

Then the door swung open. Qenet went in. Snid stood halfway across the room. He was wearing no glasses and his eyes twinkled. He waved his arms expansively. 'Come in, do come in. What an honour!' he cried. 'The Lady Qenet herself. What a lot we've got to talk about. If only I'd known you were in this sector! More lovely than ever!' he bowed. 'Do sit down. Is there anything I can do for you in my small way? Dear, dear goddess, you've no idea how gratifying it is to see another immortal in this forsaken segment of space-time. No Savrin, no Sul, no Isis and, worst of all, no Qenet. Until now, that is. But first I most apologise for yesterday's little *contretemps*. I wouldn't have *dreamt* of interfering with your old Transfer Station without seeking your prior permission. But, of course, I didn't know you were around to give it. So I can quite understand your being a little miffed with my generator equipment. And with Sir Dudley. He's a bit of an old fool, but I find him most co-operative. One has to accept the limitations of the age.' He spread out his fingers and inspected the back of his hands with a mock-regretful smile. Still smiling, he stared directly at Qenet, his head tilted slightly to one side.

The goddess smiled back at him. 'I'm fine, thanks. Just paying a courtesy visit. When I realised that you had established a base here I thought I'd come along to pay a polite call. But – forgive my asking – what are you in human drag for? Our mutual friends the Furies might take a dim view of your posing as a professor of Archaeology. Alecto's currently enforcing the Statute in this sector, I think. She's a bit easier to get on with than Tizzy or Meg – more of a sense of humour – but *I* wouldn't want to be in her little black book. And how did you raise the cash for this set-up? And what's that *muc* Krasnog's emblem doing plastered all over the place?'

'It's a long story, your ladyship. All my own silly fault, I suppose,' answered Snid with a self-deprecating smirk. 'You see, I'm afraid I've got an over-heavy touch with fine synchroherence adjustments. Perhaps you've heard about my little adventure in the Ice Age?' Qenet nodded. 'Grossly exaggerated, I assure you. But, would you believe it, my sojourn here stems from almost identical causes. A simple time-transfer, dear lady, from predynastic Egypt to the Late Neolithic. I wanted to keep a beady eye on Krasnog – the fellow does, with respect, have a few endearing features. But,'

46

he shrugged, 'you know how it is. *You*, of course, with your terapower, can so easily effect a mid-transfer correction. But poor zero-rated elves like me can't. So, here I am, stuck in the twentieth century. The benighted natives don't believe in elves any more, so I had to assume a human identity to keep myself out of psychiatric care. And once I'd done that, I'm afraid it all became too, too easy. I do hope that the Kindly Ones will take a lenient view of my peccadillo; Alecto's my favourite, as she is yours.' He bent his head towards Qenet and continued in a stage whisper. 'You'd never credit, your ladyship, the sheer, sublime ignorance of contemporary humans concerning the past. Their concept of history is a crazy combination of myth, fiction and blank misunderstanding. Do you know they don't know why dinosaurs became extinct? Or what happened to Neanderthal man. Or who King Arthur was. And as for post-glacial prehistory – they haven't a clue. "Archaeologically inacceptable" – that's what one of their experts said when their scientists produced a reasonably accurate date for the Durrington establishment. They've been churning out book after book about Stonehenge without realising that the central formations are elliptical.' He rolled his eyes in a pretence of anguish. 'Needless to say they haven't the foggiest idea about the interdimensional properties of stone circles or even of the Series I Transfer Stations. Symbiosis to them is mostly to do with lichen and nitrogen-fixation bacteria. So when I found myself stranded in this wretched and ignoble age my options were limited, to say the least. My only real choice lay between keeping to the Statute and revealing myself – as far as they were concerned – as a mythological entity, or bending the rules and posing as a human. Surely, dear lady, you wouldn't blame me for adopting the latter course?' He smiled at Qenet and cocked an eyebrow.

'So you became an archaeologist and used your first-hand knowledge of the past to make your spectacular "discoveries" in Cornwall and the Fens,' interposed Qenet. 'No doubt you've been financing this swish outfit here with other caches of treasure you've found.'

'Not entirely, dear lady,' replied Snid. 'Indeed, most of my finance now comes from the government and charitable foundations sponsored by industry. Success breeds success in this society. A few cheap export-quality Phoenician trinkets and a set of very mediocre medieval crown jewels – that's all I needed to set myself up as the country's most successful archaeologist. "Professor Snid, the Snapper-Up of Considered Trifles", one of the quality colour supplements called me. Now I get offers of assistance practically all the time. Oil millionaires, government departments, scrap magnates, car manufacturers – you name it. Next year I've decided to go over to Italy to find the treasure of Alaric the Visigoth – just think of it, the loot of Imperial Rome. And then the tomb of Hatshepsut. *That'll* make all my colleagues – or rivals, rather – in the other universities fairly puke with envy. Ham-fisted oafs, the lot of them. And do you know,' he added archly, 'I've got two dukes' sons, a prince, two princesses and three mil-lionaires' offspring among this year's undergraduates alone!'

'So now it's Snid the Snob,' murmured the goddess to herself. 'Well, congratulations on your social adaptation to the twentieth century. It's almost a pity that you'll have to give up your human guise now. Still, I'm sure you'll be glad to get back to being an elf again. With my terapower and your microelectronics skill we should be able to get Transfer Station I working in a week or two. We'll shift you back to the Otherworld and you can be your-self again, not a pseudohuman. That'll be a relief for you, won't it?'

Snid froze. Then he moved his weight from one foot to the other a few times, began to hum, walked over to the window and stood gazing over the university campus. After a few minutes he cleared his throat, took a deep breath, and began to talk musingly, as if to himself. 'Well, I wish it were as simple as that. I really do. Most sincerely. But, well, you see I've developed a conscience about this bleak and arid age. There's so much we immortals can do for present-day humans – the poor ignorant creatures. Symbiosis and all its benefits. They've lost the accumulated wisdom of the past – as one of their poets has so aptly written: "But Knowledge to their eyes her ample page, Rich with the spoils of time, did ne'er unroll." They don't know a thing about Transfer, or immortals like us. I've found it a hard life, a lone immortal among countless humans, but *so* rewarding. I feel I have a *mission* here. And now, dear Qenet, you've come back like a song.' He laughed. 'Or forward, rather. When you appeared so suddenly at that door a few minutes ago, it seemed that my prayers had been answered. By myself I can do little to help our human friends. One can't make a fire with a single stick, as they used to say in the Old Stone Age; but with you here so many things become possible. True symbiosis for one thing. You, me and a few of the human friends I have made: Sir Dudley Spatchcock, one of our most important bureaucrats – people such as he *really* rule this country, you know. Or Abdul Aziz O'Hagan, who owns the OHAG petrochemical combine. Together we would be able to do so much for this neglected age. No need to tell the others – Sul, Boan, Isis or any elves, either. Just us and a few friends.'

He turned round and faced the goddess. Qenet's expression was one of sphinx-like neutrality. Ever since the spontaneous combustion of his equipment on Overton Hill had warned him that he was not the only immortal around, Snid had been rehearsing the next part of his speech. He was deeply afraid of Qenet's notorious black rages and he had noted with relief and satisfaction that she was retaining her winsome Mode 1 form. He therefore decided to continue. 'I've given the situation a great deal of thought, my lady. Since the humans are convinced that neither of us can exist, we must remain in disguise and integrate with their social structure. With *your* charm and beauty and power and *my* intelligence and technical skill we would make an unstoppable team. My friends here will give me the resources to launch into politics and with minimal aid from you, Qenet, I could get to the top. A few trifling mishaps to my rivals – the occasional unexplained explosion, an aeroplane or two struck by lightning on take-off or landing – and I could be prime minister within a very few years. Then, at last, we could get back to something approaching the good old days of the prehistoric era.'

'And what role am I to play in this scheme?' interrupted Qenet mildly. 'Apart, that is, from knocking off your competitors? Humans only understand one kind of male-female relationship. Are you propositioning me, Snid?'

'My dear lady, how could you suggest such a thing?' simpered the elf. 'But if we could pose as a married couple it would be the perfect combination for our mutual advancement. My brains and your power. We could rule the world.'

'Big deal,' interrupted Qenet. 'But tell me, Finky, how does the Statute of Limitations fit in with all this soft-sell patter of yours?'

Snid laughed. 'As that witty fellow Lucius Apuleius said so long ago, *Quod nemo novit, paene non fit* – what no one knows about scarcely exists. Nobody would find out; not for ages anyway. There aren't any of our kind around in this sector. You might have to wear contact lenses to cover up those fascinating irises of yours, but that's all.'

'Remember what happened to Apuleius, though,' warned Qenet. 'He got turned into an ass by his girl-friend. And that would be *nothing* to what the Higher Authorities would do to you, Snid, if they ever found out. Or to me, if I co-operate with you. And their investigations are usually successful because they've got eternity. Once they've discovered what you've been up to they'll have to slam on a full-scale temporal erasure, rub it out and do a re-run. You know what sort of power that needs. Don't presume on Alecto's sense of humour either. She'll be hopping mad if you commit a

49

gross infringement of the Statute on her patch. She'll grind you up into grit and gravel; it'll be the black hole treatment for you, mark my words. Remember the Great Qualification: "Immortality is only absolute within the parameters of conventional physics." '

Snid didn't answer at once. His face showed indecision rather than fear. He rose and paced the room for several minutes. Then he stopped, sat down next to Qenet and patted her knee reassuringly. 'Have faith, my dear lady. Believe in Snid. I'm not as foolish as you think.' He wagged an admonitory finger and his voice sank to a conspiratorial whisper. 'There are ways of keeping intruders out. You must have heard of force-field isolators. They're crude but effective. Supposing, just supposing, we were to transfer in a few acquaintances of mine from other sectors – Krasnog, Grendel, Genghis Khan and Godzilla for instance – misunderstood beings all of them. Then we could bring the force-field isolators on stream and declare unilateral independence from the rest of the space-time continuum. Shut out the Higher Authorities. Give the Furies the V-sign. Who do they think they are, anyway? The three of them have been screaming around the universe and beating the living daylights out of people for too long. They're just a gang of super-annuated punks. If you ask me, it's high time someone tore up the Statute and changed the rules. Then we'll be in another ball game entirely, and a much more rewarding one, too.'

Qenet stood up. She had gone quite pale. 'Have you flipped your lid?' she inquired icily. 'I always thought insanity was a human characteristic attributable to the stresses of mortality. You just can't do this, Finky. Playing around at being human is bad enough. But transferring delusions of grandeur into the context of space-time is infinitely worse. It's unthinkable. Tizzy, Meg, and Alecto may be a trio of sourpusses, but at least they preserve some sort of interdimensional law and order. You'd never keep them out, either. Those neutrino-deactivators of theirs can make a super-nova look like a sparkler. They'll blast their way through any-thing.'

Snid stood up again and took a step backwards. The vehemence of Qenet's reaction to his plans had surprised but not discouraged him. 'I think, with respect, dear lady, that you're still too bound up with the habits and conventions of your upbringing. Revolution-ary new concepts such as mine take some getting used to, but sooner or later you'll come round to realising the truth of my ideas. The Statute has always led to inefficiency on a cosmic scale: mortals not knowing what to ask us for, elves and goddesses prohibited from telling them how to work out their problems. What we need is concerted action. A full and frank dialogue between

he?' (Thump) snarled Krasnog. 'Without telling me, his partner.'
(Thump.) 'Qenet the Fair.' (Crash.) 'Qenet the goddess of no mercy.'
(Crash.) 'Qenet *Siabur*.' Krasnog hurled the other's limp body at
the shattered remains of the cupboard. Horrified, Ben and Josie
watched as Slugwam slowly collapsed and slid down on to the litter
of glass and wood that by now covered the floor. His face came to
rest only a few feet away from them. He was unconscious and blood
was dribbling from his nose. Krasnog kicked him half-heartedly in
the ribs. 'So, Qenet, we are to meet again,' he murmured. 'So full of
pride and haughtiness. Many are the hurts Krasnog has to repay
you. My warriors dead from the kurgans of the Ukraine to the
round barrows of Wessex. For you I will pile sorrow on woe; to your
people I will bring death. Then I will deal with Snid.' He turned
and crunched his way across the room and out of the door through
which Josie and Ben had entered. All was silent except for the
sniffling of the man on the floor, who almost at once began to thresh
feebly around as consciousness returned.

Ben moved first. He got out from under the bench, grabbed Josie
and pushed her through the secret door. He had a momentary
vision of the neanderthal skeleton still grinning amiably at him.
The door whirred and closed, somehow isolating them from the
terror of the laboratory.

A second motor started up and the walls of the small room in
which they were standing began to move upwards. Disoriented,
they clung to each other, realising within seconds that they were in
a lift, going down. An open doorway appeared from the floor up.
The lift stopped. They threw themselves behind the cover provided
by three large wooden crates stacked in a pyramid by the lift
entrance. Anxiously they looked around.

They were in a spacious, well finished basement. High-intensity
light poured down from the ceiling. The room seemed deserted; it
was very long. A straight pipe of stainless steel ran diagonally
across it, encircled by metallic rings at regular intervals. To these
were fastened heavy electrical leads. At the far end of the room the
pipe was connected tangentially to a massive disc about three
metres in diameter and one metre high. This too was encircled by
rings with heavy-duty electrical connections. Ben ran over to it.
Closer inspection showed that the disc had a hollow centre, rather
like an American doughnut or a Polo mint. The steel was tinged
blue in places and smelled hot. The coils around it were actually
smoking. Ben touched one and withdrew his hand with a gasp of
mingled pain and astonishment. 'Bleeding cold,' he whispered to
Josie, who pursed her lips in mock pity and pointed to a squat glass
and steel cylinder on the floor nearby. This also was wired up and

smoking. On it was written in bright blue letters: 'Danger. Liquid Helium. Do not touch without protective clothing. Do not disconnect while in use. For cryogenic applications only. No unauthorised use under ANY CIRCUMSTANCES. Keep away.'

In unconscious obedience they directed their investigation to the other side of the room. Time was getting short and they both felt an overriding urge to get clear of this strange building with its succession of shocks and surprises. They ducked under the pipe. The rest of the chamber was empty except for two long, black, narrow box-like objects mounted on trolleys. They were equipped with elaborate stands with complex universal joints and electric servo-motors. Each was connected by coaxial cables to a smaller trolley upon which was bolted, quite unmistakably, a small-to-medium-size microcomputer. The long boxes were somehow familiar too. Ben frowned, trying to recall where he had seen one before. Josie, with characteristic practicality, craned over the larger stand and read out in a whisper: 'Laser; ruby; pulsed; nominal capacity 1 terawatt (10^{12} watts). Extreme danger to objects within total line-of-sight in Normal Atmospheric Conditions. For Experimental Use Only.' Ben glanced at the legend on the one by him. It read: 'Laser; CO_2 (I.R.); pulsed/continuous; nominal capacity (pulsed) 5 gigawatts (5×10^9 watts). Extreme danger from Black Radiation. For Satellite and Astronomical Applications Only. On no account to be employed for Terrestrial Surveying. Constructed and calibrated by Salisbury University Department of Archaeology (Palaeoastronomy Unit).'

Ben shrugged. It was all too much for him to take in. Kilowatts, yes; megawatts even. But gigawatts and terawatts, no. Then he remembered Qenet's account of the dinosaur episode at the Langdene circle. Her energy output had been 5 terawatts, or so she said. The figure hadn't meant much to him at the time, but seeing the plain figure 10^9 inscribed on the laser before him brought home some understanding of the magnitude of the power that she and, presumably, Snid, were accustomed to play around with. A thousand million watts! It was high time they made themselves scarce.

Josie caught his eye and jerked her head towards the wall. Halfway along it were painted in red the words 'Emergency Exit'. The outline of the door itself was almost invisible, but a large brass spade grip projected from its surface. Josie grasped it and tried to turn it clockwise. It didn't budge. She reversed her pressure and the handle revolved silently. She pulled on the handle and the door opened. A passageway ran about ten yards back and ended in a vertical wall against which had been set an iron ladder. Above the ladder was a translucent glass trapdoor. Josie let out a long sigh of relief and started forward. Ben's hand shot out and seized her hair. 'Watch it, for Pete's sake,' he breathed and pointed to the wall. Two sets of photoelectric cells guarded the passage. Josie's knees went weak. Ben released her, took out his handkerchief and wiped the door-handle. Still holding the handkerchief, he turned it back to its original position. Next he entered the passage and, gripping the door's edge with his fingertips, he swung it closed, releasing his hold only at the last instant before the catch snicked shut. There was no handle on the outer side. Together they crawled to the ladder. Ben mounted it slowly, followed by Josie. Luckily the light coming through the trapdoor was strong enough to show that there were no more detection devices. At the top of the ladder Ben bent his head and placed an ear against the glass. All seemed quiet. He grasped the red-painted release lever and moved it just enough to disengage it from its socket. He pushed; the panel opened. They were in the open ground behind the laboratory.

An ambulance was parked near the fire escape, effectively screening them from the main building. In an instant, and conscious only of an imperative urge to escape, they had scrambled out of the trapdoor. Ben paused to slam the outer handle shut and then joined his sister on the far side of the cryogenic store. A moment later the door by which they had originally entered the laboratory section was flung open. Two uniformed men came out. They were carrying a stretcher with a body on it. Snid was in attendance, contriving somehow to appear both worried and bland at the same time. A pretty, dark-haired girl completed the party. She seemed to be in a mild state of shock. Snid shooed her back into the passage, slammed the door in her face, and climbed into the ambulance behind the stretcher. One of the men closed the rear doors, went round to the front of the vehicle and got in. The blue light began to flash, the siren wailed and the ambulance accelerated away, its noise soon receding into the background.

The yard was empty, the laboratory windows blank. Josie and Ben backed carefully away from the store, allowing it to mask their retreat from potential watchers. Resisting the temptation to break into headlong flight, they made for the main car park. Before they could reach their conspicuous orange car they heard a shout and, turning, saw Qenet running towards them between the rows of vehicles. She arrived before they did and had the doors open for them. 'Hop in,' she commanded. 'Where on earth have you two jokers been? I've been worried to death.' She didn't seem to notice the incongruity of what she said; then she saw their faces and, without further words, handed Josie her *crème-de-menthe* bottle.

'Have a quick snort,' she ordered, 'both of you. Then tell me all about it.' She started the car, drove it rapidly out of the university campus and, once they were back on the main road, began to listen to their story. They didn't finish until the car had started its long descent into Marlborough. Qenet drove down the wide main street, selected an empty parking space in the middle of it, stopped the car and got out. 'Come on,' she said, 'time for some food.' She glanced up and down the street and led the way into a nearby café, sat them down at a table in the corner by a window, went to the counter and returned after a few minutes with a tray loaded with three delicately-balanced knickerbocker glories. She was followed by a refined-looking young lady carrying three bowls of goulash, a selection of fancy gâteaux and some coffee.

They discussed the adventures of the morning. Qenet was deeply worried by the presence of Krasnog in the twentieth century. 'That *muc*'s bad news,' she said glumly. 'I thought we'd fixed him for good back in the late neolithic. That's why he hates me so. He and his merry little gang of delinquents were difficult enough to beat even then. If Finky lets him loose with modern war technology he'll carve a bloody shambles right across this whole space-time zone. Damn Snid; *damn* him.' She poked into her gâteau with a fork, extracted a glacé cherry and crunched it up. 'But it's a relief to know that he's still as clumsy and inept as ever when it comes to synchro-adjustments. Arrived a hundred years too early, Krasnog said, didn't he?' She paused. 'Well, Josie, how does it all seem to you?'

Josie thought for a moment. 'Well, from what you've said and from what we've seen, it looks as though Snid and Krasnog have transferred up from the late New Stone Age in the hope of taking over the twenty-first century. But they've arrived a hundred years too soon and Snid's ruined the transfer circuits, so they're stranded here. They've got some powerful human collaborators but they can't get full symbiosis because they're breaking the Statute of Limitations and no goddess will co-operate. Not that there seem to be any around now except you. So they lack the energy source they need to isolate this sector of space-time from what they call the Higher Authorities. But it's clear from what Slugwam said that Snid's hoping to generate power from some sources that we don't know about; he talked about fusion reactions – that's to do with hydrogen bombs, isn't it? – and some sort of converter. But they're having serious trouble of some kind, and Krasnog's losing his patience. That's why Snid's trying to do a deal with you. He needs your terapower to enable him and his friends to take over.'

'And he's attempting to blackmail you by threatening to shut off your Transfer Stations so that you'll be stuck here for ever, like he is,' continued Ben. 'Just before Krasnog went ape he was moaning about the synchroherence circuits being blown. It's pretty obvious that Snid is ready to double-cross both you and Krasnog – that's why he didn't tell you about Krasnog's being here – or Krasnog about you. He must know that you hate each other. But what *I* can't understand is all that high technology science hardware he's got stashed in his cellar. Those incredibly powerful computer-linked lasers, and that queer stainless steel piping arrangement with the oversize annular ring at the end of it. And all that liquid helium for the electromagnets.

'I still can't make any sense out of what the little man was wittering on about – you know, plasma bottles only lasting five seconds. I've seen the plasma bottles they use in blood banks and they last for ever.' He closed his eyes tightly and rubbed his hand over his forehead. 'There's something right at the back of my mind about it. Sorry, can't remember now. It'll come back to me sooner or later,' he concluded.

They finished off their cake and began the goulash. 'We've got to keep an eye on Snid the Fink. That's for certain,' announced Qenet. 'He's playing a very murky game at the moment. That clever-clever receptionist of his told me he was going to inspect the causewayed camp at Abingdon tomorrow and then the Rollright Stones. They're up further north. I remember them being con-structed. Impressive to look at, but not very powerful – mainly because the principal formation's a true circle, I suspect. But I've never seen this place at Abingdon. . . .'

'And you won't, not now. Neither will Snid.' broke in Josie. 'Don't you remember, Ben? Old Piercy told us about the New Stone Age camps near the West Kennett barrow. The ones at Windmill Hill and Knap Hill. She said there were quite a number of other camps like them scattered across southern England, but they were rather difficult to make out because they were so old. She said some of them had been pretty well destroyed, *like the one at Abingdon.* That's what she said. Of course, she's a bit ignorant about prehis-tory, but she did seem fairly sure about it.'

'Very interesting,' commented Qenet. 'All the more reason to keep tabs on our Finky friend. We'll try to shadow him when he goes on his travels tomorrow, if that's O.K. by you. Is there an obvious route between Salisbury and Abingdon? Your modern valley roads are all different from the old prehistoric trackways I know. Could we intercept him somewhere and then follow? Let's look at some maps. Eat up your knickerbocker glories like good little children.' She giggled. 'What a crazy name!'

Back in the car they sorted out a road map of southern England. 'There's his route,' said Ben, jabbing his finger at the point marking Salisbury. 'Salisbury, Andover, Newbury, Abingdon. That means he'll use the new dual carriageway section of the A 34 up from Chieveley.' He thought for a moment. 'I know where we can pick him up. There's an unused entry road at Drayton. It's fenced off so that no traffic can get into it. We could park up it just off the northbound carriageway and wait for Snid to pass us. If he's in one of the green Range Rovers with Krasnog's sign on the side we should see him easily. Then Qenet can use her built-in computer or whatever it is to follow him. We'll have to keep well back, though. Our demon chariot's not exactly inconspicuous. Snid hasn't had much chance to see it yet, so he wouldn't recognise it on his tail. But he'd notice it soon enough and become suspicious.'

'Spoken like a true and mighty *laoch*,' exclaimed Qenet, clapping her hands in apparent admiration. Ben looked up defensively and, failing to see any hint of sarcasm in the goddess's face, blushed self-consciously. Qenet winked at Josie. 'I'm not having you on, old dear, honest. Humans are much better at tactics than immortals. Natural selection has made you that way. Otherwise you simply wouldn't survive in your hostile world. With us it's different; we may suffer inconvenience – but we don't die if anything drastic goes wrong. Not as long as the laws of conventional physics apply. So we tend to be a bit happy-go-lucky and couldn't-care-less. I would have taken ages to work out a plan as good as yours.' She reached back and gave Ben's hair a gentle tug. 'Don't you see that's why symbiosis works so well? You two are going to be invaluable in helping me to beat Snid and Krasnog. It's a real partnership, you see. Now let's get home. I want to watch that funny programme you keep sniggering about. You know, Monty Python's Flying something-or-other.'

DAY FIVE

By half past nine the following morning the Citroën was parked unobtrusively in the unused access road by the A 34 south of Abingdon. In the front, Qenet and Ben were peering at a half-inch map of Oxfordshire while Josie in the back surveyed the oncoming traffic through a pair of binoculars. 'Snid ought to come straight past here. Then he should turn off at the south Abingdon interchange, go into the town, follow the one-way system and come out on the old Oxford road. He needs the Radley road after that, which goes off to the right before he's out of the town. The old causewayed campsite is somewhere in that direction.' Ben followed the route on the map with his index finger. 'When he's finished there, he should come back onto the Oxford road again, pick up the A 34 at the north Abingdon entry, follow it round Oxford and up towards Woodstock. That's the – let's see – the third major intersection along the bypass. After that he's got a straight run up through Enstone. The Rollright Stones are about a mile on his left once he's passed the Chipping Norton crossroads. It's a fairly easy route.'

'Always provided we can pick him up in the first place,' interrupted Josie, who was balancing the heavy binoculars on the half-open window of the offside rear door. 'I can't see all that far down the road and there's an awful lot of traffic. If Snid comes along in the outside lane while one of those juggernauts is belting past I'll never get a chance to see him.' She squinted nervously through the glasses and readjusted the focus.

But she was either underestimating the sharpness of her vision or else she was lucky, for ten minutes later she tensed and, without moving her eyes from the road, punched Ben between the shoulder-blades. 'There's a Range Rover coming and it's a green one. Quick, get a look at it. It's just pulling out behind that container lorry. Yes, it's him, all right, I can see the Krasnog sign.' She prodded Qenet with her elbow. 'Put your foot down, hotshot; let's burn rubber.'

The car was already moving. Qenet had changed into third gear even before they were on the dual carriageway. Ahead was an enormous black articulated lorry. Beyond it, and just beginning to swerve back into the inner lane, was the green Range Rover. 'I can see Snid,' confirmed Josie, 'he's in the passenger seat. It looks as though he's got that girl of his doing the driving for him.'

The Range Rover's indicators and brake lights came on. The lorry in front of them slowed suddenly and its driver hooted as Snid's car veered to the left. Then they were following it down the slope to the intersection underpass. True to Ben's prediction Snid's driver took the road into Abingdon. Qenet allowed two other cars to fall in behind the Range Rover before following it into the town. The vehicles entered the one-way system round the central precinct. 'Keep in the left lane,' directed Ben, 'otherwise you'll miss the Oxford road.' Qenet obeyed. To their right, and ahead of them, they could see Snid quite clearly through the rear window of the Range Rover. 'Why doesn't that girl get into the right lane?' Ben muttered uneasily. 'She'll miss the turn. Quick,' he suddenly cried, 'cross over. They're going right.'

The Citroën sheered across the road as Qenet span the wheel round. A sedate Volvo with its sidelights on fell back to make way; its red-faced elderly driver made an indelicate sign at Qenet, who waved nonchalantly back at him as his car receded from view.

They were now right behind the Range Rover, heading away from the site of the neolithic camp. Ben was nonplussed by this apparently irrational behaviour on the part of their quarry. Then the left-hand indicators flashed and the two cars branched off towards the bridge over the Thames. The signposts read to Dorchester and Henley. Qenet slowed down to allow another vehicle to sandwich itself between their car and Snid's. She trailed the Range Rover at a distance of about fifty yards across the river and out of the town. The road widened out. Several cars in succession overtook them. The slowness of the other car seemed to be deliberate. The road passed over a railway and began to slope downhill. Then, before even Qenet could react, the Range Rover flipped its left-hand indicators again and turned off into a slip road. There was a counterbalanced barrier barring access beyond about twenty yards but they went past too quickly to see whether it was being raised for Snid.

Qenet drove on for half a mile and then bumped the car up on to the grass verge. She turned to Ben and Josie. 'Surprise, surprise,' she said, eyeing them questioningly. 'What's all this in aid of?'

'Well, at least we know where he's gone,' observed Josie. 'The sign back there said Culham Laboratories. They do physics experiments there. It's government-run, not hush-hush like the atomic weapons place at Aldermaston, though. The father of one of my friends at school works there. Nothing to do with archaeology, as far as I know. What's the matter?' she asked Ben sharply. 'Swallowed your tonsils or something?' She flexed her arm preparatory to hitting him once more on the back. For Ben seemed to be choking.

'Jet,' he croaked, waving desperately at Josie to desist. 'JET.' Then, acutely aware of the lack of understanding with which he was being viewed, took a deep breath and began again. 'J.E.T. Joint European Torus. The Common Market governments are spending £300 million here at Culham to build an advanced design torus. The Russians call it a tokamak. The idea is to get some heavy hydrogen, raise it to an incredibly high temperature and use gigantic electromagnets to confine it. Then they want to pump in superheated accelerated atomic particles. The hot gas is called plasma. The magnets force it into compartments which they call bottles. Plasma bottles – *that's* what Snid's assistant was talking about just before Krasnog started to bounce him up against the cupboard. A torus or tokamak is the technical word for a disc with a hole in it. Don't you see, that's what Snid's got down in his basement. The drainpipe thing was a linear accelerator – that's to pump in the beam of particles. The liquid helium was for low-temperature superconducting magnets. Good grief, I wish I wasn't so thick! Why didn't I recognise it yesterday? There was an article in *Scientific American* not long ago all about toroidal plasma chambers. All the scientists in my form were supposed to read it. It's coming back to me now. . . .' He banged his forehead with his fist. 'Yes, now I've got it: the great difficulty is that the forcelines keep distorting and this causes the plasma to collapse. Of course! That's why Snid has come here. He wants to find out if the scientists at Culham Laboratories have found a way to stabilise the plasma bottles.'

Both Qenet and Josie were looking at him rather blankly. 'Well, come on, bighead, what's the punch-line?' demanded the latter. 'What do they use their bottles for? Nuclear fizzion?'

Ben groaned. 'For the last ten years or so, vast sums of money have been spent on trying to start a regulated hydrogen-helium fusion sequence. It's like a controlled hydrogen bomb. High temperature plasma bottles are the only thing that can hold the reaction because it's so hot. When it becomes possible there'll be megatons of dirt-cheap energy – just like your terapower, Qenet. The sky's the limit.'

There was a short silence. Qenet spoke first. 'So that's why Snid was so confident about getting power for his force-field isolators. And that's how he's hoping to use the Transfer Station.' She scowled. 'There'll be a dark future for this sector if Snid and Krasnog get a toy like that to play their games with.'

'But they haven't got their torus working yet,' Josie pointed out.

63

'Remember what Slugwam said about the five-second bottle being the best yet? Surely they'll have to do *much* better than that before they can get any reaction going. When are the scientists at Culham expecting to be successful, Ben?'

Ben felt a surge of relief. 'I remember now. The *Scientific American* article reckoned that it wouldn't be much before the end of the century. I suppose that's why Krasnog was so stroppy. Snid must be worried, too, else he wouldn't have come here for advice. I suppose one of his powerful friends got permission for him to see the scientists here. Perhaps we've still got some time left.'

'Don't you be too sure,' said Qenet pessimistically. 'Finky Snid's a resourceful and slippery little so-and-so. He's put a lot of time and energy into this nasty scheme of his. He needs watching. I think we'd better return to the laboratories and see if he's still there. Heaven knows what he'll be up to next.'

She started the car, waited for a gap in the traffic, and then brought it round in a wide U-turn. As they re-passed the main gate of the Culham Laboratories they could see the Range Rover parked among the low brick buildings beyond it. Qenet drove on, seeking an inconspicuous lay-by. There wasn't one, so she followed a sign showing the visitors' entrance to the JET International School nearby. She stopped the car in a parking lot which gave them a view of the road. 'This must be where they teach the scientists' children,' explained Josie. 'One of the masters came over to our school last term to gas about it. The teachers here seem to get about twice the money ours do – they pay European rates, not the English ones. Father wasn't half mad when he found out.'

While Qenet sipped from her green bottle the other two poured some hot coffee out of their thermos and drank it. None of them took their eyes off the road. Snid and his companion were not long in appearing. The green Range Rover with its black and red insignia coasted past before half an hour was up. 'Well, it doesn't look as though Finky's had much success at Culham,' observed Qenet as the orange Citroën snaked out of the car park and shot after its quarry.

This time Snid did take the Oxford road. Outside Abingdon he turned right and once more joined the A 34, heading north. He was now on Ben's predicted route again. Soon the two cars were passing the first Oxford intersection. The Range Rover, as expected, kept straight on. But once they were to the north of the city things began to go wrong again. Instead of following the A 34 towards Woodstock and Enstone, the green vehicle continued along the bypass. Its driver ignored the northbound Banbury road at the next roundabout, so now it was heading towards Bicester or

Northampton. But they had hardly left the suburbs of Oxford behind when the Range Rover veered into the centre of the road and accelerated down an oblique turn to the right. Qenet was far enough behind to follow without undue risk but she took care to keep the Citroën well back from the other car, which appeared briefly from time to time as the road curved towards the village of Islip. As they entered the main street they were just in time to see Snid's car disappear into a turning opposite the church. Ben tried in vain to locate the new route on his map. Of one thing he was quite certain: the Rollright Stones couldn't possibly be Snid's real destination – they were now much too far off to the west. It was Josie who supplied the answer to his unspoken query: 'Well, they may be out of sight, but they can only be going to one place.' As if in confirmation the Range Rover came into view along a straight stretch of road half a mile ahead. 'O.K.,' Ben said after a couple of minutes, 'don't keep us in suspense. Let's have it. Where *are* they heading for?' 'Ot Moor,' replied his sister, pointing to a road sign. 'It's a United States airbase. Went to their open day last year. Another of my friends has a father who works as R.A.F. liaison officer there. She says he spends all his time buying double-glazing for the local inhabitants so they can sleep at night.'

As usual, Josie was right. The countryside began to take on a flat, low-lying aspect. The distant edge of the plain was marked by a ridge of hills several miles to the south-east. They skirted Charlton-on-Otmoor and soon afterwards a high double perimeter fence topped with barbed wire came into sight. Beyond it they could make out the misty outlines of five or six enormous light-blue hangars. The barrier ran alongside the road for a couple of miles; from time to time it vanished behind the tall hedges, now brown, orange and yellow with autumn leaves.

Just beyond Murcott a large notice had been erected some yards back from the wire. 'U.S.A.F. Ot Moor', it read; 'Strategic Air Command. 14th Bomber Group, 256th Squadron. Commanding Officer Col. M. Minderbinder. No unauthorised admittance. Guard dogs patrolling. All visitors report to main gate.' The road went on past an isolated church, over a small bridge and round a sharpish bend. About a hundred yards further on they saw the green Range Rover standing empty, parked up on the grassy verge beside a gap in the hedge. Qenet drove by without slackening speed; she passed a few cottages and then bumped the car down a bridle path to the left. She stopped behind some bushes. They all got out cautiously. 'Snid and Co. can't have moved far from their car,' said Qenet. 'They must be somewhere behind the hedge back there.' 'Probably going to the loo,' muttered Ben. 'But I suppose we had better check up. I'll go over and see if I can find them. Qenet, perhaps you'd better stay out of sight, since they know you.'

He began to walk as inconspicuously as he could towards the Range Rover. But before he could approach it Snid and his driver emerged from the undergrowth and climbed in. The engine started and the vehicle drove on to the main road. Ben moved on to the verge to make way for it and was rewarded by a smile and a wave from the dark-haired girl as she accelerated past him. No sooner had Snid's car disappeared from view than the Citroën nosed its way on to the road and drove off after it.

Ben was left alone. Philosophically he walked to the gap in the hedge beside which the Range Rover had been parked. He could now see that the hedge itself had been cut down to give clearance to a set of overhead electricity cables and that the trees behind it formed a hollow square which screened a small enclosure.

This was in turn surrounded by a chain-link fence. Even before he was near enough to read the warning notice Ben had recognised it as an electricity substation. Inside the wire were three grey-painted step-down transformers. But what caught his eye was a dome-topped container about the size of a dustbin which had been placed between two of the transformers and connected to one of them by a heavy insulated cable. It too had been painted grey and there was some writing on its side. Ben strained his eyes to read it and could just make out the words 'University of Salisbury. Department of Archaeology. Atmospheric C_{14} Sensor. Danger – High Voltage. Do not touch.'

He considered the situation for a moment. Then, with a quick glance around to make sure no one was looking, he climbed over the padlocked gate, carefully avoiding the barbed wire on top of it. He crossed over to the Carbon 14 sensor and examined it. The dome was evidently detachable: two lug-like handles were mounted opposite each other where it joined the cylindrical body. A broad arrow indicated that it should be rotated anticlockwise to open. Ben hesitated for a few seconds as he remembered the war stories he had read about booby-trapped devices, took a deep breath and eased the dome round. It freed itself with a slight click and Ben lifted it gently away from the rest of the sensor. Three objects were revealed inside the case. One of them was immediately recognisable as a U.H.F. transmitter, with its aerial aligned in a southerly direction and inclined upwards at a shallow angle. Attached to this was an elaborate-looking Geiger radiation counter. The third component was more puzzling; it was a matt black dish about a foot in diameter. A short stalk projected from its centre to end in a ball of black plastic. It was pointed across the road in the general direction of the airfield.

Ben studied the assembly in front of him. The dish and its stalk, he realised in a flash of inspiration, was a sensitive directional microphone. He had seen reporting crews using ones like it on T.V. In no way could it have anything to do with the detection of atmospheric carbon. The device was designed to monitor sounds from the airbase and relay them to a receiver located somewhere further south. It was all very mystifying. Ben carefully replaced the protective dome and locked it in place. He was climbing over the gate of the substation when a loud hoot almost made him lose balance. Alarmed, he looked up to see the car draw up beside the trees. He jumped down and ran over. Josie held a door open for him and he climbed inside. 'Drive off,' he whispered, and put a finger to his lips. Fortunately Qenet understood, and the car moved away. Once they were out of the range of the microphone Ben asked her to stop and explained about what he had found. 'Snid had to leave it there because he needed the substation's electricity to power his relay transmitter,' he concluded. 'But what I can't understand is why he wants to bug the airbase. What's so special about it?' As if in answer a low grating roar began to blot out his words. Two planes howled along the runway. They rose steeply, wheeled overhead and then, sounding like mammoth cement-mixers, slowly flew away to the east. 'F111s,' explained Josie for Qenet's benefit. 'Swing-wing fighter-bombers. According to Katy – that's my friend – they're equipping them with those new hydrogen bomb cruise missiles. Top-secret, she says. The idea is that they can go in low under enemy radar, launch the missiles, and then beat it back here. If there's anything left to come back to, that is. According to her the Russians have got at least one intercontinental missile targeted on the base here. She calls them nukes, because they have nuclear warheads.' She gazed at the sky and shivered. 'Let's move on a bit,' she said; then she frowned. 'Someone was talking about using a nuke only the other day. Who was it?' Her face cleared. 'I remember – Snid's assistant. He said that if their torus didn't work, they could use some gadget or other which could be triggered off by a small nuke. That's what he said, didn't he?' She turned to Ben for confirmation.

Ben nodded. 'Yes, he was talking about using an M.H.D. converter. It would be a much less advanced system than the torus. The idea is to explode a nuclear device down a mine and use the plasma it creates to generate a great surge of electricity. M.H.D. stands for magnetohydrodynamics. I don't understand how it works, but it's in the exam syllabus. It's the basis of that anti-satellite system they were talking about in *Panorama* the other week. You hook your M.H.D. converter up to a heavy laser and burn out the target with a pulsed beam.'

There was silence as the three of them mentally digested the implications of Ben's words. 'You're not going to tell me, are you,' continued Ben slowly, 'that Snid's hoping to heist a nuclear warhead in order to power that terawatt laser of his? The way they guard those things makes the Bank of England seem like a holiday camp. He'd never get within a mile of a nuclear store without being electrocuted, mined, eaten by guard dogs and shot.'

'We were much nearer to a couple of them a few minutes ago,' retorted Josie with some asperity. 'They went overhead at 300 feet in those F111s. Katy says they always keep a few armed planes up in the air so that if war broke out and their base was destroyed they could still fly off and obliterate their targets. And every so often they have a red alert.' She was warming to her subject now. 'The publicity man told us all about it on the open day. The S.A.C. headquarters at Denver put all their bases on a war situation without telling anyone it's only a practice. All the lights go on, the sirens start to scream and they scramble the planes. It's only when they're on their way to the targets that they recall them. It's a fail-safe system, or so they say. Snid's sensor device would pick up all that noise, wouldn't it? It would tell him that the loaded F111s were taking off. All he'd have to do then is to hijack one while it's on the flight path to its target. Much easier than breaking into the weapons store at the airbase, if you ask me.'

'I suppose your gabby friend hasn't told you which route they take?' Ben inquired with irony, 'Have the K.G.B. offered her a job yet?'

Josie was unabashed. 'Don't be daft, she's only passing on common gossip. As a matter of fact, baby brother, she did say something about that.' She considered for a moment. 'Yes, now I remember. The pilots keep moaning about the Swedes and their new Viggen interceptors. Sweden's a non-aligned nation, so they shoot at *anyone* who crosses into their airspace. Even NATO planes have to fly round the country. So they have to go straight up the North Sea and round the North Cape of Norway. Then they have a run-in to Murmansk, where the submarine bases are. The aircrews don't like the first part of the trip – they call it Blowtorch Alley because of all the oil-rig flares they keep having to dodge. They fly low, you see, to keep under the radar. I reckon all Snid's got to do is put a gun on a rig and let one of the F111s have it as it goes past. You know, like they shot up the Tie fighters in *Star Wars*.' Another thought struck her. 'What about those dirty great

68

lasers he's got in his bunker at Salisbury? Couldn't he use one of those?'

Ben, too, was quite excited now. 'Yes, of course. It would be the 5-gigawatt infra-red laser. Infra-red light can't be seen and it will penetrate fog and mist. A 5-gigawatt pulse would cut through just about anything. But you can't go blasting planes out of the sky without someone noticing. Snid would need the co-operation of a whole oil-rig crew – and he'd need frogmen to retrieve the H-bomb from the plane once he'd brought it down.'

Qenet's clear voice interrupted their conversation. 'Who owns these oil rigs?' she inquired.

'Most of the big oil companies do,' explained Josie. 'They pipe the oil back to the shore and flog it to the rest of the world so that we go short whenever there's a crisis. You ought to hear Mum and Dad go on about it.'

'Does the name OHAG mean anything to you?' asked the goddess. 'Snid boasted about a crony of his called O'Hagan. He said he was boss of some oil outfit called OHAG. If he really is going to try and shoot up a nuclear bomber over the North Sea it would make sense for him to use an OHAG rig as a base.'

'OHAG's one of the big oil multinationals, all right,' said Ben, 'and those rigs are certainly equipped with heavy-duty generators, lifting gear, cutting equipment and diving bells. If OHAG really have got a well or two in the North Sea and their owner's one of Snid's gang, it would make it much easier for him to bring down an F111, rip out the bomb and lift it to the surface. And everyone would be looking for a submarine or a battleship. They wouldn't suspect an international oil company whose rig just happened to be in the neighbourhood.'

There was silence in the car again. 'And what can we do about it anyway?' said Josie, after a while. 'We've no real evidence. If we went to the police, they'd fall over laughing. Two schoolkids and a hippy girl – they'd most likely put us in prison for malicious defamation of character. Anyway, what could Snid want an H-bomb for? O.K., he digs a hole somewhere, buries the bomb in it and somehow gets a whopping great pulse of electricity. What can he do with it? Switch on the Blackpool lights? Blow all the fuseboxes on the National Grid?' She looked round challengingly.

Ben shrugged. Qenet, however, tapped her nails on the dashboard for a moment or so. 'I think I know,' she said. 'Perhaps I ought to have levelled with you before, but I wasn't certain – not until just now. You would know too if you'd ever seen a Series I Transfer Station trigger mechanism. The old Series I stations were operated by a coded signal transmitted in coherent light on to a continuum interface stabiliser. As soon as I saw Snid's people playing around with a laser at the Sanctuary the other day I knew what he was up to. He's aiming to reactivate the Transfer Station at West Kennett. Laser light is coherent: those sun-discs we saw at Devizes Museum were components from the original trigger mechanism which used to be sited over at the Sanctuary on Overton Hill. That's why Snid wanted to borrow them. He's an elf, so he must know all about synchro-electronics. While the long barrow is kept closed by the Ministry of Ancient Monuments he'll try to patch up the silicon microcircuits inside the gatestone there. He'll get his collaborators to cart the great blocking stone out of the way, install his terawatt laser at the Sanctuary, feed the synchroherence code into the computer and then detonate the bomb. That is, if he can't get me or the torus to produce the power he needs in a more civilisèd way. Even with one terawatt he'll blast open the interlock circuits for anywhen he likes. Heaven know what he's got lined up to come through from the other side. Krasnog's army of cut-throats, Genghis Khan and his murderous gang. He said something about a monster or two as well when I saw him yesterday. Those disaster movies they keep showing on television will seem like *The Muppet Show* compared with what'll happen when Snid's superthugs get going.' She ran her fingers through her long blonde hair and tugged it in exasperation.

The others listened to her in silence. The thought of a horde of rampaging savages emerging from the long barrow to conquer the world for Snid and Krasnog was not a happy one, to say the least. Then Ben spoke. 'If you really look at things logically,' he began, 'Snid's threat to bring in a load of savage barbarians from the past doesn't really make sense. Are you sure he wasn't having you on, Qenet? Don't you see – people like Genghis Khan were horrific enough at the time, but no modern army would be worried. They'd mow them down with twentieth-century weapons. The government would simply send up tanks from the ranges on Salisbury Plain and massacre them. If you ask me,' he added darkly, 'Snid and Krasnog won't bother about the past. They'll try and get some ghastly doomsday weapon from the future. A neutron-beam projector or a neuronic whip or something even more unpleasant.' He paused, searching his mind for other horrid sci-fi contrivances.

Qenet gazed speculatively out of the window. 'That figures; I hate to say so, but it does. Everything begins to make sense if you look at it that way. Suppose you're right. Suppose Snid's arranged for something nasty to be parked at the barrow site at some date in the future. All he would have to do is transfer it back to the present.

70

That would explain why he's so desperate to get the Transfer Station working again, and that's why a single energy pulse would be sufficient. Once he's got his doomsday weapon he'll be able to knock off some more nuclear bombs. Then he'll blast open the interlocks again and transfer a fusion plant back from the future. After that he'll connect up his FoFIs – force-field isolators – and try to make this sector immune from Otherworld interference. Intra-continuum piracy – it's been tried before, but not often. Snid's risking even more than I thought. The Furies are always on the lookout for that sort of caper. Tisiphone, Megaera and Alecto – three ladies with black bats' wings and snakes in their hair, though of course they can mutate into any form they like. They're a sort of multidimensional riot squad – Hecate's the goddess in charge of them. Tisiphone and Megaera – Tizzy and Meg to their friends and acquaintances – are operating in other sectors at the moment. Alecto's been assigned to this one. She's what you'd call a real tough cookie, though I'll admit she's got a sense of humour: a smile on the face of the tiger, so to speak. If *she* finds out about Snid's little game he'll have had his chips. Once and for all, immortal or not.' She drew a finger across her throat. 'But in the meantime I'd like to settle my own account with our Finky friend. No one, especially a pretentious half-goblin like him, makes a takeover bid for Qenet's Transfer Station. Or talks to her as though she were some glamorous bovine battery with no other purpose than to supply his squalid schemes with terapower.' She was becoming quite worked up. Josie and Ben were conscious of their hair beginning to stand on end: for a few seconds she hovered on the edge of a transformation into Mode 3. Then with an effort she stabilised herself. 'Well, there's really only one thing to do. We'll have to complete our symbiotic grouping. Snid and his human rabble won't stand much chance against that. Not unless he can find a goddess to work with him, and he'll never do that, though,' she added thoughtfully, 'he might get one of those tarty water-sprites to co-operate. Anyway, we need an elf. You two have quick human wits and an intuitive sense of self-preservation; I've got terapower. A friendly elf will have the technical skills to manipulate synchrocircuits. He'll also be able to give us the low-down on Snid: elves are a clannish lot, and generally know what each other is up to.'

She considered for a moment. 'Mar Ten's our best bet. The most talented silicon-quartz elf in the business. He did a lot of work for me during the second and third millennia BC and knew all the top people at the research centre down near Stonehenge. I came to know him fairly well. Rather a quirky sense of fun, though – I told

71

you about the tyrannosaur trick he played at Langdene, didn't I? The trouble is he's really hooked on dinosaurs. Always zooming back to the Cretaceous, and that's a Long Leap – 65 million years or more. Transfer Station I couldn't handle that – even if it were in good nick, which it isn't, and even if I waited until next Samain, which I can't. And anyway Snid's persuaded that damned Ministry of his to seal it off.'

So it was in a rather dispirited mood that they drove home; even Qenet's handling of the car seemed unusually staid. Each was thinking about Snid and Krasnog. Could their schemes be as monstrous as the evidence seemed to indicate? Or were they all allowing suspicion to run away with their imagination? And did the other side really hold the initiative?

By the time they reached home they had all come to the same answer on question one – probably yes. Snid and Krasnog had been too explicit (or too unguarded) in what they had said over at Salisbury. The answer to question two was less cut and dried: with Snid's perverse intelligence, Krasnog's ruthlessness and the resources of their influential human supporters they seemed to possess indisputable advantages. Josie and Ben, considering matters separately, concluded that, given time, Qenet would probably win. Her combination of steely beauty and shattering reserves of raw energy was profoundly reassuring. But both of them were depressed by their own inadequacy. Against the allies of Snid they felt they counted for little.

Qenet saw things differently. Her wider experience of people – both human and immortal – had given her a different scale of values. For materially successful humans she had little respect. Their coarse and aggressive ways she found repulsive; their claims to intellectual competence she rejected absolutely. Over the centuries she had witnessed too much crass idiocy and callous selfishness on the part of prominent humans to have any regard for their value as allies. She greatly admired Josie and Ben: their quick and penetrating intelligence she valued far more than the costive minds of those who had decided to support Snid. What made her so gloomy was her own inability to deploy her terapower. The cosmic system of checks and balances which allowed her to radiate almost unlimited quantities of power but withheld from her the ability to utilise it was all very well, she reflected, in a situation where nobody cheated. Secretly she had been deeply humiliated by Snid's apparent capacity to substitute inanimate contrivances based on heavy hydrogen atoms for her own energy. Her apparent incapacity to do much about it roused her to fury. Several times on the way home Ben and Josie felt the now familiar static charge that

72

denoted Qenet's inner emotion. Snid might hold the initiative; possibly he might even win the battle. But neither was prepared to rate his ultimate prospects of health and happiness very high.

DAY SIX

The next morning they were sitting round the breakfast table explaining the situation as they saw it to Ben and Josie's parents. Perhaps it was the combination of Qenet's matter-of-fact air and her demonstrably superhuman powers that persuaded the grown-ups to accept without demur a tale which, on first sight, appeared to combine the least credible elements of a fairy story with those of hard-core science fiction. What was needed, Qenet kept insisting, was the assistance of a friendly elf, Mar Ten preferably, so that the full advantages of symbiosis might be achieved. But with Snid and his bureaucratic friends shutting off the circles and long barrows in the area (all of which were pretty dilapidated and unserviceable anyway) the problem was how to get back to the Cretaceous Age to recruit him.

'Well,' observed Mr Jameson, 'none of *your* Transfer Stations would have been much good for that job, anyway. All the chalk-lands were at the bottom of the sea during the Cretaceous, weren't they? That's how the chalk was deposited. You need somewhere on good old-fashioned igneous or metamorphic rock if you don't want to get your feet wet when you arrive.'

'Go on – we're not *that* stupid,' answered the goddess. 'All A.A.A. circles have integral ambient stabilisers. They make sure that you end up at approximately the same temperature and humidity as you started in. They'll divert the interface automatically. That's why we got a tyrannosaur at Langdene, not a plesiosaur or something like that.'

She tapped her teeth reflectively with her thumb-nail. 'But you may have a point about rocky sites, especially if they're on high land. There would be fewer humans around to smash them up, especially in your foul modern climate. Now Savrin had a few Pi 3s over in the west. Mostly pretty late ones – Bronze Age. They used quartz microcircuits, not silicon like mine. Some of those might still have a transfer capability of some kind. They were tucked away inside the great curve of her river, over beyond the Long Mountain. I'm sure she wouldn't mind my using one of them if it's in working order.' She stood up. 'Have you got a map of the west?' she inquired. 'And are there any genuine archaeologists who could tell us about the stone circles over there?'

Ten minutes later the breakfast things had been cleared away and they were grouped around a small-scale motoring map of southern England and Wales. 'There's Savrin's river,' said Qenet, tracing the long course of the Severn up from the Bristol Channel through Worcester and Shrewsbury. 'Look, that's the great curve I was telling you about.' Her index finger moved round to the west of Shrewsbury and then south-west towards Welshpool, Newtown and Llandiloes. 'And there's the Long Mountain,' she pointed to the characteristic outline of the Long Mynd. 'Look how empty the country is over there. Hardly any towns or roads. Perhaps they've left the circles alone after all.'

Josie scrutinised the map closely. 'So you reckon Savrin's circles ought to be somewhere between, say, Bishop's Castle and Shrews-bury itself. What we need is a larger-scale map. The Ordnance Survey 1:50,000 would do. Let's go to Swindon and have a peek at them in Smith's there.' She looked in a superior way at Ben. 'You can make yourself useful for a change and go to the library to see if they've any books on circles and barrows and that sort of thing. We'll meet you at the coffee-bar by the Brunel Centre afterwards.'

Ben, without quite knowing why, repressed an impulse to throw something at his sister. With what he hoped was an air of aloof dignity he left the room, took the car keys from their hook in the kitchen and went to back the Citroën out of the garage.

Once at Swindon they left the car in the gloomy recesses of a multistorey park. Josie and Qenet went to the map shop while Ben, still slightly resentful, made his way to the library. There he inquired about archaeological books dealing with stone circles. The assistant, an enthusiastic-looking lady in her thirties, answered his query without hesitation. 'You want Thom,' she announced. 'Tom who?' replied Ben, rather puzzled. The librarian laughed indulgently. 'Alexander Thom,' she explained. 'He's spent a lot of his life surveying prehistoric stone circles and working out their astronomical significance.' Leaving the counter, she led Ben towards one of the less frequented areas of the room. She stopped in front of a row of books classified in the low 920s, paused for a moment and then seized one and pulled it out of the shelf. 'Here you are: *Megalithic Sites in Britain.*'

She handed him a slim, light blue book with a fanciful picture of Stonehenge on the cover. Ben glanced at it and began to thank her for helping him, but she was already halfway back to her place at the counter. He wandered over to one of the tables and sat down. The book appeared to be a fairly detailed one. He flipped through the chapter on statistics and astronomy; the section dealing with the mathematical background he examined with greater care and was rewarded almost at once by two diagrams showing circles with slightly flattened circumferences. His eye caught the familiar Greek letter π somewhere in the text. He lost it and had to read almost the entire page systematically before he relocated it near the bottom:

$$perimeter/MN = \pi^1 = 3{\cdot}05$$

So *that* was what the Pi 3 circles Qenet was always talking about looked like! The diagrams showed two types: one had a Pi value of slightly over 3, the other slightly below. The book gave constructional details of both. Qenet had said there might still be a few circles in Shropshire, so Ben turned to the list of sites. Location after location was given, each with its grid reference and a coded description. He scanned the list carefully. There was a Pi 3 circle at a place called Loch Nell – obviously in Scotland. Next came a succession of ordinary circles, another Pi 3 at Aviemore – again in Scotland – and then five more with D-prefixes to their grid references. Ben caught his breath; two of them were in Shropshire: Mitchell's Fold and Black Marsh. Ben closed the volume, noticing as he did so that his hand was trembling a little. By confirming Qenet's account of the geometry of the circles the book had forged another link between the misty past and the statistical and scientific present. For a moment Ben felt that both were within his grasp and that he could almost will himself from one dimension to the other. The sensation faded; he walked over to the counter, had the book stamped, left the library and made his way to the elevated market. There was no sign of Qenet or Josie at the café but he found them nearby examining the dresses in one of the boutiques. Assuming as deadpan an expression as he could, Ben told them about the Shropshire circles. Josie responded by pulling a cerise-coloured Ordnance Survey folder out of her anorak pocket. 'Here's the map of the Ludlow area,' she volunteered. 'It's the one with the Long Mynd on it. Let's have a coffee and check the grid references from your book.'

Sipping coffee, they examined the map. Both the circles were there, Black Marsh practically on the northern edge of the map and Mitchell's Fold about a mile and a half to the south-west of it. A footpath joined the two sites. To the west the Severn meandered briefly onto the map and then vanished off it in the direction of Welshpool. On the right the long line of Stiperstones lay diagonally across the landscape, almost bracketing the circles. Further east the close-drawn contour lines of the Long Mynd dominated the scene.

Qenet drew the map towards her and began to fold it. The other two looked questioningly at her. She stood up. 'Right, let's get going,' she began in a matter-of-fact way. Then, noticing the surprise on their faces, she paused. 'What's the matter? It's only about 140 miles to Shropshire from here, isn't it? Say about two and a half hours by car. We'll be back in time for tea.'

'Oh no,' groaned Ben, 'not another kamikaze performance!' Josie remained seated. 'And what about your little trip to the Cretaceous?' she inquired. 'Isn't that going to take time? I mean if we've got to grub around in the swamps trying to find your friend Mar Ten. . . .' She stopped speaking as the implications of the situation struck her. 'Heavens, it'll be like organising a full-scale jungle expedition,' she cried. 'And what about the monsters – you know, carnivorous dinosaurs and all that?'

Understanding dawned on Qenet's face. 'Don't be a unidimensional nitwit,' she chided. '*If* either of the Shropshire Pi 3s works – and it's a big if – we'll return without any temporal discontinuity. People could actually be watching us from outside the circle for the whole time without noticing anything unusual. We could spend years in another sector of space-time but we'd return at the exact moment we left. Unless I make a goof, that is.'

'You mean like Snid?' queried Ben.

The thought didn't appear to worry Qenet. 'He's an elf, I'm a goddess. I've got an inherent store of energy, he hasn't. So I can carry out course corrections while I'm in transit. Snid has to make all his settings beforehand and is committed to a fixed course as soon as he triggers the interface stabilisers. Now don't you worry; interdimensional travel is as easy as falling off a log – for goddesses. Once we've found a serviceable Transfer Station, that is. So are you lot coming or not?'

They paused only to buy a selection of sandwiches, cakes and coke at the café before leaving. Qenet took the opportunity to replenish her supply of liqueur at an off-licence and soon they were speeding along the old Roman road that runs straight from Swindon to Cirencester and thence to Gloucester. For the first part of the journey they were travelling through the prosperous and picturesque countryside of the upper Thames valley and the Cotswold Hills. The Citroën seemed to spend most of the time in the offside lane, overtaking long lines of lorries and then cutting back in the nick of time as Qenet's split-second reactions warned her that disaster, usually in the form of an approaching articulated lorry, was imminent.

Once they had crossed the Severn, however, the nature of the terrain changed. Villages were small and relatively scarce; traffic was thin. The colour of the earth changed to red and ahead the great mass of the Malvern Hills appeared to the left and slowly swung across the horizon as the road worked its way westwards through Ledbury. There was a fast, uneventful run through to Leominster and beyond; at Aymestry the mountainous border hills began to close in. The land became even emptier and the cultivation line fell back from the hilltops, which were bare or covered with dark coniferous trees.

Now they were approaching their destination. Josie and Ben began once more to feel the electric tension radiating from their companion. As the car drove past Bishop's Castle the western scarp face of the Long Mynd came into sight. Just beyond the small village of Lydham Qenet slowed down. The road edged its way round Corndon Hill. 'Next left for the Mitchell's Fold circle,' called out Josie, the map balanced on her knees. 'Look, here's the turning, opposite that old mine.'

The car swerved off the main road. 'Watch out for a sharp right turn,' warned Josie, 'and follow it round. Then go straight ahead when the road bends left. There's a track that leads up to the circle.

Qenet followed her directions and soon the car was bumping along a well defined lane. She adjusted the suspension as it lurched through the mud and puddles. After about three hundred yards she drew in to the verge, pulled on the handbrake and switched off the engine. Everything at once seemed very quiet. They all got out. In silence they marched together up the slope, not knowing quite what to expect. An iron gate barred the way; they opened it and went through and at once they were in another, wilder type of country, full of grass, bracken and sheep. Some way ahead a notice-board stood out on the skyline. They reached it and discovered they had arrived.

The circle stood on a rough plateau; to the left the ground dropped away into a bracken-covered coomb, while on the right it rose gently towards a horizon dominated by the jagged quartzite crags of the Stiperstones. The circle itself was surprisingly small – not comparable in size even with the inner circle at Avebury – and the upright stones, with one exception, were set low into the ground: some of them showed only a foot or so above the short grass. It was quite impressive in a rather rustic way. But did it work?

Qenet had gone straight to the stone immediately opposite the single tall upright one and had taken a careful sighting over them both, kneeling on the ground to obtain an accurate view. She moved anticlockwise to the next stone and did the same thing. She was smiling as she came over to Josie and Ben. 'The circle *feels*

O.K.,' she explained, 'and the two energising alignments are still spot on, believe it or not. There's an equinox setting on the highest of the Stiperstones and one for midwinter's day lined up on that quartzite pillar over there.' She pointed to an isolated tower of rock some distance to the south. 'So let's give it a whirl. Would you please mind standing over there, about ten yards outside the circle. It should be quite safe.'

Hardly knowing what to expect, the two of them moved over towards the notice, upon which was perched their sole spectator, a sagacious-looking crow. Qenet meanwhile walked over to the tallest of the stones, reached up, and placed her hand firmly on the top. For a moment nothing happened; then, with a sharp bang, a blue high-tension spark shot across the gap to the next stone. It wavered, stabilised and jumped to the stone beyond. Within a few seconds the spark had jerkily travelled round almost the whole circumference of the circle. Only the space between the stone Qenet was touching and the one on its left remained unbridged. Qenet, keeping one hand in place, stretched out her other arm and tiptoed sideways. The spark detached itself from the last stone and moved hesitantly towards her. Halfway across the gap it stopped. The goddess closed her eyes in concentration and the spark began to move again. It paused, retracted slightly and then leapt forward to touch Qenet's outstretched fingers. She drew it gently towards the large upright stone. There was another sharp crack and all the stones were linked by a continuous thread of blue ionised air which fluoresced quite distinctly in the weak autumn light.

Qenet withdrew her hand from the rock, walked to the edge of the circle, ducked under the band of light and beckoned to Josie and Ben. 'The circle's operational now,' she explained, catching a wisp of hair which had fallen in front of her face. 'Whoever built it certainly knew his job. Not many circles – even Pi 3s like this – could be expected to retain an interface capability for 3,000 years. There's been some loss of fine adjustment, but I reckon I can compensate for that. Well then, who's for a trip to Mar Ten's hideout in the Cretaceous?' She lightly kicked them to their feet. 'Be careful of that spark,' she called out unnecessarily as she turned back to the circle, 'and hurry up please, or someone'll see the pretty lights and tell the police a UFO's landed.'

Whether she intended it or not, Qenet's light-hearted approach to time travel had a reassuring effect. Together Josie and Ben crawled into the circle; the crow watched them for a moment and then launched itself into flight. 'All aboard the *Skylark*,' cried Qenet, 'those that don't come back don't pay.' She gave a wicked grin and clapped her hands.

79

Nothing happened. Literally nothing. Josie, glancing back beyond the circle, noted, with a delayed sense of astonishment, that the crow was hanging motionless in the air. Everything went silent as daylight drained away. The circle, its stones still connected by the shimmering thread of incandescent blue, remained unchanged. Outside, all was blackness. The ground within the circle was no longer covered with turf; it had taken on a glassy texture. Radial lines could be traced beneath its surface from each stone to the centre.

Qenet was standing at the point of intersection. She had kicked off her crimson slippers and appeared to be absorbed in a complicated sequence of disco dance steps. Sparks fizzed between her feet and the floor as she gyrated with an abstracted, almost expressionless look on her face. Seeing the bewildered air of the others she laughed ruefully. 'Rotten contacts, I'm afraid. Conductivity isn't all it should be. All this arcing's giving me dreadful pins and needles. Hang on a minute.' She sat unceremoniously down and peered at the surface of the intersection area. Then she placed both hands palm downwards upon it, took a deep breath, closed her eyes tightly and pushed hard. There was a *ping* and the intersection began to radiate a uniform dull red light. Qenet rose to her feet. The light spread gradually outwards along the radial lines until it reached the stones. 'Now watch this,' she called out. 'It's my favourite party trick – all the fiery force of immortality. Snid would give his ugly fangs for it, and so would your physicists.' She clapped her hands again while Josie and Ben watched closely, not having the foggiest idea what would happen next. Then the goddess began to glow; the light within her intensified and lit up the whole circle. Her green dress tinted her radiance and the embroidery on it showed in dense dark lines – as did her golden bracelets. Her bare feet, arms and face shone with a slightly pinkish tone. Most striking of all, Qenet's eyes showed up black except for the pupils, which glowed with twin beams of ray-like intensity. Her fluffed-out hair added a halo effect. It was all most impressive, disconcerting even. 'Talk about the bionic woman,' muttered Josie, but she was careful to say it too softly for Qenet to hear. Ben just stared; a half-forgotten phrase from an old Greek story had come back to him – something about the flashing eyes of Athene. Had all the goddesses of the ancient world appeared like this to their human acquaintances?

Qenet's glowing glance swept towards him and Josie. 'Sorry about the pyrotechnics,' she said in a conversational tone. 'They're only phenomena connected with terapower radiation. I must say you two have taken it all pretty well. I've known older people than you fall on their faces and howl at the sight of it all. What I'm doing now, in case you haven't guessed, is initiating a microstasis megannular transfer – known in the space-time trade as the Long Leap. Rather like a fast rewind on your tape recorder. It's an enormous distance by any standards – about 65 million years. On maximum power this circle should take about an hour of apparent time to get back that far – about a million years a minute. We're already well beyond the Ice Ages and you wouldn't find any men around if we stopped now. Only extinct mammals and a few hardy beasts like crocodiles and sharks.'

'I read an S.F. story once,' began Ben, 'where someone went back to the Cretaceous Age to hunt dinosaurs. When he returned to the present he found that something he had done back there had changed everything. The language was a bit different, and so was the political situation.' Josie interrupted him. 'Yes, suppose we stopped off in 1066 and clobbered William the Conqueror as he was crossing the Channel – surely a lot of things would be different in our own time. No Norman Conquest. Perhaps everyone would be speaking Anglo-Saxon when we arrived back. We wouldn't be able to make ourselves understood.'

'And if Snid is planning to transfer a doomsday weapon back from the future to help him take over this space-time sector, he'll be doing the same sort of thing,' broke in Ben. 'Is that why you're so cross with him?'

Qenet glanced in his direction, forcing him to shield his eyes with his hands. 'Have you ever heard of a modern Celtic poet named W. B. Yeats? I was reading in one of your books that he wrote his own epitaph:

> Cast a cold eye
> On life, on death.
> Horseman, pass by.

That's really the golden rule for anyone who's moving around in space-time. Legalistically speaking, there are three categories of interference you can cause if you're in an alien sector: Inconsequential, Deviant and Catastrophic. If you take things easy and keep in the background, what you do is generally inconsequential – the future's hardly affected at all. But if you start mucking around with the situation, your behaviour becomes what is technically classed as deviant, and it's up to any right-minded immortal – like me – to put a stop to it pronto. Snid's position is in this category at the moment. Now should he actually start trying to rule the world, he moves automatically into the catastrophic grade. The life of anyone – even an immortal – who gets into that sort of situation is likely to be nasty, brutish and short.' She paused. 'I've told you about the Furies. They turn up quite often in classical mythology. So does their boss, Hecate. One of their jobs is to locate anyone guilty of castastrophic infringement of the Statute and give them the works with their neutrino-deactivators.' She looked directly at Ben, 'Tell us what a neutrino-deactivator does, Einstein.'

Ben blinked and considered. 'Atoms are almost entirely made up of empty space,' he replied. 'Electrons are kept relatively distant from the nucleus by mysterious sub-atomic particles called neutrinos. If there weren't any neutrinos the positive protons of the nucleus and the negative electrons would slam together. The whole atomic structure would collapse, like it does in a neutron star. A handful of compacted atoms would weigh a billion tons. If they're compressed further, beyond what's called the Schwarzschild radius, they become so heavy that even light can't escape from them. That's what a black hole is. Black holes are like cosmic whirlpools. Once anything's inside the event horizon of a black hole it's trapped for ever.' He made a sketchy bow. 'Is that O.K.?' he asked.

Qenet made an equally sketchy curtsey. 'Brilliant; the Furies carry neutrino-deactivators, so all they've got to do is press the button and pow! – a mini black hole. It's the only way of dealing with immortals. One of our basic rules says that immortality is only absolute within the parameters of conventional physics. Forget that, cause a catastrophic anomaly, and you get the black hole treatment. It's happened before. There's a bit in the Bible about a god who vanished without trace – it's in the Book of Elijah, I think.'

'But even supposing the Furies catch up with Snid at some point in the future,' Josie said, 'surely he'll have altered world history and that would be irreversible. If we're going to quote poetry, how about that bit which runs:

> The Moving Finger writes; and, having writ,
> Moves on: nor all thy Piety nor Wit
> Shall lure it back to cancel half a line.
> Nor all thy Tears wash out a Word of it . . . ?'

'Well, it's not *really* like that, you know,' replied the goddess. 'It only seems as though the past can't be changed. It can be, but it's appallingly expensive and highly embarrassing to the Higher Authorities. What happens is that when a catastrophic infringement of the Statute is discovered they have to initiate what's known as a total segmental re-run. The whole sequence of events has to be reversed between the correction and interference points, wiped clean, and then allowed to go forward naturally. Think of the energy input that requires! The orbit of the earth has to be reversed for a start; and the moon's as well. If the worst comes to the worst, I suppose I'll have to call in Hecate or one of her riot squad – although usually they've got an uncanny ability to detect trouble early on. But even so it would be something of a black mark for me. We're supposed to keep our own territories in order, without help from outside.'

She yawned and stretched. 'Almost there,' she said. 'We're slowing down now.' Qenet's inner glow faded and then blinked on and off several times as she made some final temporal adjustments. 'That should do it within six months or so,' she announced, and clapped her hands.

The red lights went out; only the blue barrier spark remained. Sunshine from an unclouded blue sky burst into the circle, and with it a sharp smell of seaweed.

The stone circle now stood on an outcrop of rock overlooking a long curving bay. Long regular waves of clear greeny-blue were breaking upon a beach of white sand. Behind the beach lay a grassy plain which stretched towards a range of low mountains a few miles inland. The plain was dotted with clumps of palm trees, some of which came almost down to the shore. The light was dazzling and the whole scene had a surrealistic clarity about it. It was totally unlike the steamy swamps of enormous horsetails and tree ferns which Josie and Ben had been expecting. Josie noted with astonishment that they were once again standing on grass – an unworn, fine-leaved bowling green type of turf. A common-or-garden grasshopper landed from nowhere onto one of her shoes; she bent down and collected it on her finger. The creature shuffled up her hand, gazed expressionlessly at her, jumped and vanished. She wondered for a moment if Qenet had got it all wrong and whether they had simply shifted in a geographical sense – perhaps to the Caribbean or to some other exotic corner of the tropics. Yet she sensed a difference that went beyond the crystalline vividness of the landscape. Ben, too, wore a puzzled expression; without warning he flexed his knees and jumped upwards . . . and upwards, or so it seemed. Actually he only rose about two and a half feet, but that was high enough to solve the problem immediately. 'The gravity's weakened,' he exclaimed disbelievingly, and turned to Qenet for an explanation.

'You've got it in one,' she said. 'How else do you think our furry friends up there could leave the ground?' She pointed inland above the mountains where some birds, high in the sky, were slowly gliding in their direction. Only they weren't birds, Josie realised with a shock. They were pteranodons and very, very big indeed 'Are they dangerous?' she called anxiously to Qenet, for by now the great flying animals could be seen quite clearly. The encyclopedias of the twentieth century had not done justice to them. They seemed to combine the elegance of Concorde with the effortless flight of a glider. Their wing-span was that of a medium-size plane; and they were covered with a greyish-white down.

Qenet wandered over. 'Nothing to worry about,' she answered her companions. 'They're far too fragile to risk attacking land animals our size. But they're inquisitive beasts. Watch this one!' A pteranodon had broken away from its fellows and was coming down towards the circle in a wide spiral. It sailed over at about fifty feet and even at that height it made Josie and Ben duck. They caught sight of one dark, intelligent eye as it cocked its crested head towards them and they heard the thud of its wings as they slowly began to flap. The animal swung round towards the sea passed over them again, and began to climb steadily. Within a few minutes it had rejoined the rest and apparently communicated to them the inedibility of the group below. At once the flock (squadron seemed a more apt collective noun) began to disperse. Only one remained, hanging far above and almost invisible against the intense glare of the sky.

Ben settled himself comfortably on the grass. 'How's Mar Ten going to find us?' he asked. He didn't feel particularly worried, for the Cretaceous Age seemed to hold a number of interesting possibilities. He watched his sister, who was executing a series of mid-air somersaults.

Qenet didn't reply at once. She waited as Josie landed fair and square on top of Ben, bounced and rolled to a halt near the highest stone of the circle. 'Mar Ten will have rigged up a network of sensors. Bound to have. He's probably been televiewing us ever since we materialised.' She waved into the distance and blew an airy kiss. 'And anyway our barrier spark must create enormous static interference. He'll be able to get a fix on our position without any trouble. And talking of barrier sparks,' she continued, 'I think that it may be just as well we've left ours on. Look over there, along the beach.'

Ben glanced beyond Qenet. At once he appreciated her concern Stomping purposefully in their direction was – unquestionably – a *Tyrannosaurus rex*. A sharp intake of breath on his right indicated that Josie had seen it too. There was no mistaking the

eature. This one, unlike the pteranodon, did look exactly like the
lustrations they had seen: greenish skin, small forelimbs with
ngered hands, massive rear legs and a long tail stretched out
gidly to balance its blunt head. For some reason Ben had always
upposed that the great bipedal dinosaurs had hopped along rather
ke kangaroos. This one certainly didn't. It plodded forward
ft-right, left-right along the beach. Every so often it would stop,
ase itself back on its tail, and rear upright to get a better view.
nd there was no doubt what it was looking at. Them. All the
orrific facts that he had learned about the dinosaur came back to
en with a rush: forty feet long; high as a house; six-inch fangs; a
eight of nine tonnes. The largest, most fearsome carnivore ever to
xist.

The animal reached the edge of the sand and lumbered on to the
ock about a hundred yards from the circle. Ben blinked twice and
ried to refocus. Again, something was wrong; his mind and his
res seemed in conflict. Then he realised with relief that though
ie approaching animal was a tyrannosaur all right, it was only a
ttle one. Against the long perspective of the beach it had been
ifficult to gauge its size. Now, as it came closer, they could see that
was only about four and a half feet high, though its long tail
iade it seem larger. The beast advanced steadily to within a yard
r two of the barrier spark. Then it sat back on its tail and, head
slant, gravely surveyed the three people before it.

The tyrannosaur had a surprisingly humanoid appearance,
lought Ben. Its eyes certainly lacked any suggestion of reptilian
uelty. They were of a soft brown colour and had an intelligent,
ven roguish twinkle. Ben's battered credulity gave another lurch
s he noticed that around its neck was a broad green ribbon with a
eatly tied bow in front. Josie, always a sucker for animals, edged
ast Ben. The creature grinned amiably at her, revealing a glisten-
ig array of stiletto teeth, and winked. It gave a languid wave of its
ft paw, which it held out in the obvious expectation of a hand-
iake. The gesture captivated Josie. She ducked under the barrier
nd took the proffered limb. The tyrannosaur grinned even more
nd tilted its enormous chin upwards. Josie gently withdrew her
and and took hold of one of the loose ends of the bow. The ribbon
ame undone; attached to it was a folded sheet of paper. Josie
:anned it and handed it to Qenet. 'It's for you,' she said, and
eturned at once to her new friend. The goddess took the sheet. Her
ame was written on the outside in a neat uncial script. She
nfolded it and read out aloud:

Dear friends, my name's T. Rexy Pooh,

I've come to say hello to you,
And welcome to the late Cretaceous –
Where the climate's fine but beasts voracious.
Please follow me now to Mar Ten's pad
But best watch out for mum and dad.
They've got appalling appetites –
And no respect for human rights!

Typical elvish rhyme!' she commented. 'They can't ever resist it
Always lapsing into verse – just like Shakespeare's heroes.' Sh
turned to T. Rexy Pooh. 'O.K., chubby-chops, take us to you
leader.'

T. Rexy gazed appraisingly at the goddess for a moment, then h
grunted in an affirmative sort of way, tilted himself forwards an
downwards, and jerked his tail clear of the ground. With surpris
ing agility he pivoted round through 180 degrees and began t
march back the way he had come. Qenet, Josie and Ben followed
Hundreds of feet above them the pteranodon banked round in
curve and spiralled once or twice to keep the group more easil
under surveillance. Otherwise nothing much seemed to mov
except the waves, and even they were very regular and wel
behaved compared with the boisterous seas of the twentieth cen
tury. There was no driftwood on the beach and really not muc
seaweed either. It was a sunny, unspoilt world of bright san
rustling palms and blue sky. And everywhere an unnatural clarit
of colour.

Three hundred yards out to sea several large fish flipped them
selves into the air. Their appearance was followed by that of wha
appeared to be an animated submarine periscope. T. Rexy stoppe
dead and fixed his bull-terrier eyes upon the object, which rapidl
submerged again. 'Plesiosaur,' said Ben. 'Nessie's great-great
grandfather,' added Josie. They were now nearing the rocky head
land at the end of the bay. Ahead of them the footprints of T. Rex
continued in an undeviating line towards the ridge. The group lef
the beach and began climbing. At the top the world seemed t
change. They were standing on the rim of an impact crater abou
three-quarters of a mile in diameter. The asteroid or meteor whic
had caused it must have hurtled down to smash more or les
exactly on the shore line, so that a semicircular bay had bee
gouged out of the land on one side while a ring-shaped barrier ree
had been thrown up from the sea bed on the other. A shimmerin
hemispherical object was anchored in the centre of the lagoo
which had thus been formed. The abnormal symmetry of th
lagoon itself and unworldly appearance of whatever it was in i
gave the whole scene a distinctly science-fiction edge. But T. Rex

seemed used to it; he plodded stoically across the shattered rocks and down once more on to the beach. He made a bee-line for a stone about five feet high which stood just above the tide-line. When he reached it he stopped and, with an air of satisfied achievement, eased himself upright. He eyed his three companions benevolently. Qenet spoke first. 'That's a standard force-field interface out there.' She jerked her head towards the object in the bay. 'Half of it must be under the sea. That's bound to be where Mar Ten hangs out, but don't ask me how we're supposed to get in. Terapower would punch a hole in it, of course, but I'm not paddling out there to try it. The Cretaceous water might be nice and warm, but it's got too many nasty cold beasties in it for my liking.'

As if to underline her apprehensions another plesiosaur (or it may have been the same one) stuck its long neck out of the water and fixed all of them with a speculative and predatory eye. T. Rexy Pooh snorted loudly, leaned forward and began to lumber towards the sea. The plesiosaur crash-dived out of sight but Rexy didn't stop. He charged straight into the water, and, apparently unimpeded, ploughed out of sight beneath its surface.

The others felt isolated and vulnerable and edged closer together. T. Rexy's headlong rush into the hostile ocean appeared incompatible with his previous sedate and gentlemanly behaviour; then his head emerged from the waves and for a moment he stood chest-high in the sea, an interrogative expression on his face. To the bemused minds of the humans this now-you-see-me-now-you-don't behaviour seemed just another inexplicable feature of the fantasy world into which Qenet's arrival had pitched them. But to Qenet, long familiar with elvish technology, it made sense. She stamped her foot in exasperation, winced as she felt the hard stones of the beach and cried, '*Muc* that I am! A few days in your low-technology age and I'm out of touch already! What that dear intelligent animal is trying to tell us is that there's a force-field spur locked on to this stone. That's how we're supposed to enter *chez* Mar Ten.' She tossed her hair and trotted briskly towards the waiting dinosaur. T. Rexy turned and vanished again beneath the waves. Qenet followed him. Ben and Josie found themselves alone by the water's edge, self-conscious and not a little worried. Josie put her foot into the water and withdrew it; Ben, taking a deep breath, marched resolutely in. The water rose to his knees and then to his waist. It didn't feel cold – or wet, for that matter. Fear of being marooned on a prehistoric shore had overcome Josie's reluctance to get her feet wet and she was close behind him. An arm appeared a yard ahead. Ben wondered dimly if it ought to be holding a sword or something. The index finger beckoned; he took another deep breath and advanced a few paces. The arm vanished and almost instantaneously he felt a sharp blow behind his knees. They buckled and he collapsed downwards through a thin curtain of water into a dry and airy tunnel. Qenet was sitting on the sand; she had just grabbed a pair of disembodied legs which immediately proved to be those of Josie, who fell on top of her. Further down the tunnel T. Rexy Pooh was waiting expectantly. Josie and Qenet disentangled themselves and the whole party advanced down what appeared to be a tubular corridor of non-reflective glass.

Soon the sandy floor had vanished and water surrounded them. About ten feet above the tunnel they could see the patterned surface of the sea, while below the rocky bottom shelved away into the depths. A dark shape flashed between them and the sunlight. It corkscrewed round, braked and hovered a few feet outside the interface. Once again they found themselves under the cold gaze of the plesiosaur. It was a strange animal – an enormous glinting turtle-like body with spade-like flippers at each corner and a long, snaky head. It made no attempt to break through the force barrier to get at them but cruised alongside on a parallel course. T. Rexy studiously ignored its progress until it was almost opposite him. Then he exploded into activity: his muscular tail threshed sideways at the sea monster, slammed into the side of the tunnel and penetrated far enough to land a hefty clout on its neck. The plesiosaur struck back repeatedly, its eyes glittering balefully from their sockets at the top of its head, but could only dent the shield. T. Rexy, secure in his immunity, pressed his snout against the interface, bared his teeth and grunted what must have been a selection of dinosaur invective at his foe. After a minute or two the latter withdrew several yards, exhaled a cloud of bubbles and rose to the surface. It hovered above the tunnel and then shot off across the bay. T. Rexy withdrew his head, stretched his neck and, with a leer that could best be described as self-satisfied, resumed his role as guide. The brief incident had been a mixture of slapstick comedy and horror movie – with enough of the second element to make the humans greatly relieved to see ahead of them the silvery surface of Mar Ten's place. There must have been some sensing device in the passage, for on the approach of the party the mirror-like disc became translucent and then transparent. T. Rexy barged straight through and the others followed, to find themselves at the bottom of a huge sphere about thirty yards in diameter. The sea-green floor sloped upwards and away in all directions until it merged indistinctly with the diffused blue light coming through from the sky above. Suspended in the centre of the sphere, looking like a large moon in its diminutive sky, was a second force-field. The whole set-up was overwhelming. It gave the impression of a technology so far in advance of the twentieth century as to be beyond comprehension.

A tall figure in nondescript green was standing just inside the entrance. After ceremoniously shaking the dinosaur's paw (or was it hand?) Mar Ten turned to Qenet. 'Greetings, my lady. Welcome to my modest shack, and welcome to your friends, too. At your service, as ever.' The elf gave a quick smile; his spare, tense build and the bright green of his eyes gave an impression of mercurial dynamism. There was friendliness but little deference in his style and he listened impassively as Qenet gave a summary of the events leading up to their visit. When she had finished he strolled over to T. Rexy, patted his head once or twice and looked directly at the group before him. 'I'll come, of course,' he said. 'A formal request by a goddess for help from the Sidhe can't be refused. And anyway it's Finky Snid's delinquent behaviour that's at the root of the problem. He's always been a pain, that one. I reckon he's picked up a few goblin genes from somewhere.' Then he gave a sudden fey smile. 'But I'll make one condition and one only. T. Rexy must come with me. I'm not leaving him here alone. The poor deluded creature thinks I'm his parent and it would do terrible things to his sense of security. Anyway, the presence of a dinosaur will make the twentieth century a much more respectable place, won't it, Rexy?' The animal cocked its head and gave a ferocious grin. The elf turned to Josie and Ben. 'I expect her ladyship told you I'm a bit of a Cretaceous freak. Frankly, the idea of trekking forward 65 million years for a slugging match with Snid and Krasnog doesn't exactly grab my imagination. Those two were made for each other, when you come to think about it. Sooner or later they were bound to team up. But I reckon they've pushed their luck too far this time.' He glanced at Qenet. 'Are you sure it wouldn't be better to call in Hecate's riot squad?' The goddess shook her head. 'I don't want the Furies on my patch. At least, not in the line of duty. It's our Transfer Station that Snid's messing around with, Mar Ten. So it's up to us to straighten the misbegotten *muc* out. What he needs is a one-way ticket to the Precambrian: nothing there but green slime to keep him company. My terapower and your time-transfer circuitry should do it, provided we've got some low human cunning to help us.' She flashed a smile at the others.

Mar Ten gave a shrug of assent and turned to Josie. 'How do you like dinosaurs?' he inquired. 'Do I detect a kindred spirit? You'll find T. Rexy Pooh perfectly tame. He doesn't bite friends – at least not seriously. Tickle him under his chin and he'll be a friend for life.' Josie did so and the dinosaur stretched its head upwards and

89

snuffled with pleasure. Mar Ten grinned at her. 'Saved him from one of your ancestors,' he said. 'He was in the last egg of an abandoned clutch. The night-racoons had eaten the rest. I brought it back here and he bashed his way out almost at once. Saw me and thought I was his mother – or father. That was a year ago. He goes off now and again by himself to hunt brontos, but he's not much of a predator. Intelligent, though, even for a dinosaur. Small brain, but superb natural microcircuits.' He prodded T. Rexy in the ribs. 'Come on, let me show you all my place; and you can tell me about the twentieth-century world as we go round. I hope you don't mind my saying so, but that end of the continuum has always seemed a bit drab to me. Rotten sub-Atlantic climate, highish gravity and no symbiosis. I've never stayed long anywhen after the Romans appeared on the scene. What's your stage of technical development? Steam? Internal combustion? Atomic fission? Qenet tells me controlled fusion isn't due for some time yet and your people haven't a clue about terapower storage. That means your scientists can't even be thinking about interdimensional transfer yet, which makes things a good deal easier for Snid.' He paused. 'Something the matter?'

Ben had lurched forward uncontrollably. He would have fallen flat on his face had not the elf caught him by the arm. Now he stood, eyes shut, swaying. 'It's your floor,' he gasped, 'it looks uphill but it feels flat. It makes me feel all dizzy.'

Mar Ten continued to hold his arm. 'Keep your eyes closed,' he advised, 'and let me lead. You'd better stay still,' he called over his shoulder to Josie. 'I've had this trouble with guests before. It's my fault, I should have warned you.'

The two of them began once more to walk ahead. This time Ben had no difficulty in keeping his balance. It was Josie, who, watching them, had to grab T. Rexy. For as they progressed farther from the entrance it became obvious that they were beginning to climb like flies up the curving inner surface of the spherical force-field. But they remained upright and continued to stroll upwards until they were directly opposite; suspended, apparently, from the bluish ceiling. Mar Ten looked down at Josie, Qenet and T. Rexy and waved cheerfully at them. Josie's senses went into reverse. Now it appeared that *she* was up above and the others down below – or was she? Ben, his eyes now open, seemed equally disoriented. He sat firmly down on his part of the ceiling – or was it floor?

'It's nothing to worry about,' called out Mar Ten, 'though I admit it does take a little getting used to. It's called an integrated gravity field. Think of your own world. You don't have to go uphill to

Scotland or downhill to Africa, do you? The earth seems flat, though you know it really isn't. It's the same here. It's just that your eyes associate slopes with increased gravity and your muscles automatically compensate. Come on, be brave and run over to us.'

T. Rexy galloped off at once with Josie hanging on to his neck for dear life. Qenet circumspectly followed. The floor's colour changed from green to blue and soon they had rejoined the others. Above them still hung the central force-field, set against the greenish ceiling. Mar Ten took a small silver square from his pocket and pressed it. The blue surface around them dimmed, the green translucence above cleared and they were looking up into the vast aquarium of the sea. A shoal of vivid blue and yellow fishes was streaming upside-down round the dome. Three or four fearsome dolphin-like creatures were tearing in and out, long saw-tooth jaws snapping and large staring eyes locked on to their prey. 'Din-din time for the ichthyosaurs,' murmured Qenet. Mar Ten touched the square again and the dome once more became cloudy. 'Integrated gravity gives marvellous spatial economy, you know,' he continued. 'In a normal room the walls and ceilings are just so much wasted space. But in here the walls and ceilings are floors as well. Over 6,500 square megalithic yards all on one level. And up there,' he glanced at the concentric inner force-field suspended above them, 'that's my bedroom, bathroom, kitchen and store.'

Ben was suitably impressed. 'How on earth do you get up there?' he asked 'there's no stairway.' By way of reply Mar Ten rose gracefully into the air, drifted upwards for a few yards and, apparently without hindrance, vanished through the force-field above them, only to reappear head first a second or so later. 'Come on, Rexy, show them how to come upstairs,' he called, pointing at the dinosaur, who jumped and rose like a lumbering lunar kangaroo to join his master. The elf pointed to each of the others in turn and one by one they felt the gravity around them die. Each rose silently into the spheroid above.

Inside, it was rather weird. They had all apparently ascended into the kitchen, which occupied a full quarter of the inner globe and, unlike the area outside, definitely had a floor area, which was of course curved, and two walls, which converged to form an attic-like ridge above them. The whole room was shaped like a segment of an orange. A row of storage units with work surfaces and some rather elaborate cooking and refrigeration appliances lined the walls, though gaps had been left for access into the neighbouring compartments. 'Bedroom to the right, loo to the left,' Mar Ten explained. 'The doors are just weak fields, so you can walk straight through them. Have a look around, by all means. But first

91

we'd better feed T. Rexy.' The dinosaur was already sniffing eagerly around what seemed to be a large freezer. Mar Ten looked at Josie. 'Be my guest,' he said. She nodded and pulled open the store. A number of enormous chops were hung inside like coats in a wardrobe. T. Rexy waited with ill concealed impatience for Josie to heave one off its hook, then he leant forward, took it in his mouth and tramped over to place it on one of the surfaces. He prodded and pushed it on to what must have been a cooking element of some kind and then, with obvious concentration of mind, he placed his left paw on one of the switches. The surface glowed briefly and T. Rexy reached forward, seized the meat, and sank his teeth into it. *Scrunch, gulp, scrunch, gulp,* and it was gone. 'Just like the last sitting at lunch time,' observed Ben, impressed nonetheless by the efficiency of the dinosaur's masticatory equipment.

Mar Ten's inner rooms took some getting used to. Like the kitchen each was shaped like the segment of an orange or a slice of Gouda cheese. The curvature of the floor was much more evident than it had been in the large outer shell, so the effects of the gravity field were all the more confusing. Moving across a room was like walking in a treadmill; the walls and floor seemed to shift but one always stayed at the bottom. Leaning forwards, back or sideways at steep angles, everyone else seemed on the point of sliding down. But they didn't.

As they entered the living-room, Josie and Ben quickly began to realise that force-field physics had applications beyond anything they had so far imagined. There were no chairs, no bed, no carpets – or nothing that could be so described in material terms. A resilient field covered the floor, shimmering with a golden transparency. Faint mists of spectral colour showed where other fields projected upwards to support anyone who cared to flop into them. The sensation of doing so was a novel one – something between sitting on a sag-bag and relaxing in a mudbath. Since there was no upholstery to tear or springs to break, the force-field furniture held immense trampoline potential. The fun began when Ben, seized by a quixotic impulse, grabbed T. Rexy's tail and tried to swing him round by it. The whiplash response sent him in a parabola which ended in an area of restful greenish light that presumably served as a bed for Mar Ten. He slammed into it, was catapulted sideways, rebounded painlessly off the floor and came to rest embedded in a rosy aura of colour near the apex of the room. Josie and Qenet, diving to avoid him, found themselves sinking voluptuously into half-perceived areas of softness. T. Rexy, sensing a new game, took an ungainly leap after Ben and landed upside-down in the middle of a violet haze not far from his assailant. Mar Ten, appearing on the scene from the kitchen, gave a grin of malicious joy, and, taking the control plate from his pocket. pressed it hard. The fields instantly solidified, embedding all four in a firm, unyielding grip. Mar Ten sauntered over to the immobilised dinosaur, leant over and began to tickle his feet. T. Rexy tried to writhe out of his way but could only manage a protesting wriggle. He turned his brown eyes pleadingly upon his tormentor, who relented, pressed the plate again, and deposited everyone on the floor.

It was some time later that Qenet, remembering the gravity of her mission, reminded Mar Ten that they ought to be thinking of getting back to the circle. She was a little apprehensive about taking T. Rexy back to modern times, but Mar Ten was adamant. When she pointed out to the elf that he could easily synchronise his departure with his return (thus not appearing to have been absent at all), he merely smiled cryptically and made no reply. The goddess shrugged, though she could not refrain from observing rather acidly that a neat track of tyrannosaur footprints across the twentieth-century landscape would do terrible things to the assumptions of contemporary biologists.

So as the party made its way back through the sea-tunnel and along the beach it included T. Rexy Pooh, who once again led the way with Josie and Qenet. Behind came Mar Ten and Ben, discussing the finer points of jet-age technology. Above them the pteranodon hung on station in the cloudless sky. From the crater edge they caught sight of what must have been a small herd of brontosaurs in the middle distance. Otherwise there was little to indicate that they were not in some unfrequented tropical paradise of their own time sector.

They reached the stone circle and entered it. Qenet regenerated the isolating spark, clapped her hands to activate the stasis field and stood on the central intersection making polite conversation as the ages sped past. She seemed even more relaxed on the return journey than she had been on the outward one. Josie, with an uneasy vision of distraught parents and country-wide police searches, inquired as nonchalantly as she could whether there was likely to be any difficulty in synchronising their arrival with their departure. She had worked out in her head that a 1 per cent error on Qenet's part would bring them back just over half a million years too soon – or too late, while a lapse of only twenty-four hours by earth time would be quite sufficient to cause all manner of dire consequences. Mar Ten reassured her. 'Goddesses have a built-in sense of timing,' he explained. 'You and I have got super locomotor precision – we can touch the tip of our noses with our eyes closed. I wouldn't trust her ladyship to do that – she'd probably give herself a black eye – but she's endowed with a sense of timing that makes a cesium clock seem like a sundial. She'll get us back within a microsecond, you'll see.'

Nevertheless there was a slight tension in the air as Qenet stepped off the contact plate, smiled at her companions, and disengaged the stasis field. Josie thought she could discern the slightest hint of reproach in those triple-irised eyes as, in the growing light outside, she made out the immobile airborne shape of the crow that had taken off a moment before they had set out 130 million years – or was it only an instant? – previously.

The bird vanished over the bracken-covered landscape. A chill wind blew down from the Stiperstones; everyone suddenly felt cold – and heavy, too, as modern gravity asserted itself. Qenet neutralised the spark and they stepped out on to the footpath that led back to the road. There was no one in sight, which was just as well considering that T. Rexy's first action was to advance in an elaborately casual way towards a group of surprised-looking sheep who were standing at the edge of the bracken. The dinosaur, gazing narrowly at his intended prey, was within a few feet of the sheep before, with a concerted spring, they stampeded away. All of them that is, except one. For T. Rexy, with a powerful forward leap, caught it in his massive jaws, broke its neck with a quick toss of his head, and gave it the *scrunch, gulp* treatment, wool, bones and all. Ben, hardened though he was by the dissection work of his biology course, turned rather pale. Josie actually screamed. T. Rexy merely looked rather pleased with himself.

Mar Ten and Qenet were intrigued less by Rexy's behaviour than by the humans' reaction to it. 'Don't worry about the wool and bones; dinosaurs have stones in their guts to grind up their meals. That sheep will be mincemeat in no time at all,' began the elf, mistakenly relating their concern to Rexy rather than to his victim. Qenet simply commented that they would see sights more bloody than a sheep-killing if they were going to shear the belted and bristling Krasnog to the bone and burn his brains for fire-fat. Used to the goddess's picturesque Celtic turn of phrase, Ben and Josie took scant notice of this remark at the time. Later they were to realise its real significance.

The party reached the car without further incident. They heaved and prodded Rexy into the back. He accepted this treatment with equanimity, hiccuped once or twice, and settled down for a snooze. They covered him with their anoraks and hoped that no one would notice his tail draped casually over the rear seat. Then Mar Ten insisted upon a quick examination of the Citroën. He became quite

enthusiastic as he bent over the flat-four engine, tut-tutted disapprovingly at the distributor and the battery, and was about to
ease off the air filter to get a better view of the carburettor when
Qenet pointedly suggested that it was high time to start back.

Indeed it was, for as Ben was banging the bonnet shut a Land
Rover lurched round the corner, turned up their track, and
bounced up to them. On its sides were painted the initials of the
Ministry of Ancient Monuments and in the back could be seen
some bundles of chestnut palings. The vehicle drew level and
stopped. The driver opened his window and gave a friendly wave.
'Is there a druids' circle hereabouts, bach?' he asked Josie. She
pointed towards Mitchell's Fold. 'Their high and mightinesses in
London are wanting us to fence it off,' explained the man. 'And the
one at Black Marsh, too. It's the vandals, they say. Load of old
cobblers if you ask me. Nothing better to do than send out orders
telling us to stop people going where no one goes anyway. Stupid
nits.' He nodded affably, let his clutch in with a jerk, and drove off
along the track.

Qenet gazed after him, the fingers of her right hand tapping
sharply on the roof of the car. 'Snid's mob move fast,' she commented bitterly. 'They're obviously trying to cut off access to all
workable Transfer Stations. It's high time he and Krasnog were
given their come-uppance.' She jumped into the driver's seat,
revved up the warm engine and banged the car into gear almost
before the others could get in.

She drove all the way home though it became more and more
evident during the journey that Mar Ten was itching to have a
spell at the controls. At Leominster they refuelled and Josie and
Ben bought some fish and chips while Qenet introduced the elf to
the pleasures of tippling. Rather to their surprise he asked for
some solid food as well. 'I've got to keep my protein level up, you
know,' he explained. 'I'm not just an electric battery like her
ladyship here.' Rexy snored gently through the whole trip, while in
the back seat Mar Ten cross-questioned Ben about the workings of
the car, which fascinated him as much as it did Qenet. But his
inquiries tended to be technical ones and Ben soon had to extract
the maintenance manual to help him out with the answers. What
was the compression ratio? the elf wanted to know. How much
torque did the motor deliver? What was its working temperature
and fuel consumption? How did the ignition system work and how
effective was the automatic vacuum timing adjustment? All these
questions and many more showed a knowledge of theory which
went well beyond Ben's. At length Mar Ten finished his interroga-
tion, admitting somewhat grudgingly that the twentieth-century

95

petrol-engine seemed to constitute an ingenious use of what amounted to a rather unlikely and esoteric energy source. He also hinted broadly that he could hardly wait to get started on some improvements of his own devising.

The Citroën howled across the country: Ledbury, Gloucester, Cirencester, Swindon, Marlborough. Only when they were almost within sight of Silbury Hill did Qenet slow down and ease the car to a stop between a group of towering transcontinental lorries parked outside a transport café near the Ridgeway crossing. They all got out and trooped in.

A strikingly good-looking dark girl was standing behind the counter. Her black hair hung in a curtain of slender plaits around her shoulders and she was wearing an expensive-looking red velvet jump suit. She smiled in a friendly way as the party ordered varied combinations of chips, baked beans, peas, eggs, sausages and bacon. 'Anything to drink?' she inquired. 'How about a green goddess for you, love?' She put the question direct to Qenet, who for a moment seemed shaken out of her habitual composure. She gave the waitress a hard, appraising stare. 'O.K.,' she assented, 'all round, please.' The dark girl glanced briefly at Josie, gave a conspiratorial wink and busied herself with bottles of *crème-de-menthe,* cointreau and gin.

Clutching their refreshment the group moved towards an empty table. No one appeared to take notice of their unusual beverages. A driver at the next table munched through his steak, eyes fixed on the inner pages of the *Star*. Outside, lorries and cars sped past in the gathering dusk. Mar Ten caught Qenet's eye. 'Things have changed quite a deal since we were here last – and not much for the best,' he said, perusing the graffiti scrawled on the dusty side of a lorry in the yard outside, which concisely enumerated the fate awaiting Swindon United at the hands (or rather feet) of Oxford. 'I suppose the Hill's still there, isn't it?' He craned his head to the right. 'I thought that Rex and I could hole up there for the time being. There should be plenty of room.' He turned to Josie and Ben. 'How close does this road go to Silbury? I wouldn't care to risk taking a dinosaur across too much open country. I'm sure he would have a most unfortunate effect upon the morale of the present inhabitants if he were spotted.'

They assured him that the old Roman road almost touched the hill. 'Of course,' added Josie, 'it's fenced off like the other prehistoric monuments. The government people say it was being flattened by children running up it and rolling down the other side. After 5,000 years, too,' she sniffed in disapproval. 'But Qenet's blasted a hole in the fence and the place isn't guarded anyway.'

96

Ben seemed worried. 'It'll be horribly cold and damp in there,' he said. 'The tunnel's been shut up since they dug it out ten years or so ago. And from the photographs I've seen there's not much space in there either. I wouldn't like you or Rexy to get bronchitis or rheumatism.'

Mar Ten smiled. 'No problem. We'll use the old control chambers. Sil Hill is what you might call a prototype Series 1B Transfer Station. Not one of our most outstanding successes, really; it didn't replace the long barrows – *they* went on for another five hundred years or more before the Series II circles began to make them obsolete. But her ladyship' – he nodded at Qenet – 'always had a sneaking affection for it and we engineered things so that her river came out from its base. She considered that the local humans needed some compensation for all the work they put into it for her. Very pretty it looked when we'd finished. Ferns, moss – a grotto, I think your word for it is. But then the Romans came along, slapped their causeway right across it and converted what was left into a well. That's another story, though. What I'm talking about is the subterranean chambers. We ripped out the interface generators and junked them but left the support systems in the control and transfer modules. Then we set permanent deflection fields up around them. That makes them virtually undetectable, at least to people at your level of technology. All we've got to do is relocate the entrance and smuggle Rex in.'

By now they had finished their meal; they rose and wandered out to the car. As they got in, Josie heard a snuffle and, looking in the back, saw Rexy's eye peeping out from under the anoraks. The dinosaur's tail began to thump as she patted his head.

Just past Silbury, Ben, who was driving, took the car off to the right of the road on to the bumpy and deserted forecourt of what had once been a petrol station. They got out and scanned the gloom for signs of life. There were none. Cautiously Mar Ten opened the tail door and, still keeping Rexy draped in Josie's bright blue anorak, heaved him on to the ground. Josie couldn't help giggling at the sight of him standing there like some prehistoric version of Paddington Bear. Ben and Mar Ten were already moving off towards the hill. 'Get that animal behind a bush or something quickly – before a car comes along,' shouted Ben hoarsely. Qenet and Josie each took an arm and, with the dinosaur waddling between them, followed the other two up the slope. Once they had found the fence, Mar Ten led the way round to the Avebury side of the mound, away from the road. He stopped and waited for the others. 'The main entrance was somewhere around here, wasn't it?' he asked Qenet. The latter frowned, then nodded. 'There's been quite a lot of earth-slip since I was here last, but I'm fairly sure the opening is pretty close. Everybody stand back, please – it's time for more party tricks.'

She shooed the others about ten yards down the slope, returned and faced the side of the hill. Then she raised her hands level with her head and cupped them as though she were grasping a large ball. Once again she began to glow; but this time nothing else happened. After half a minute or so she switched off and turned to Mar Ten. 'It's not working,' she called. 'Are the receptor circuits blown? Or are the relays jammed? Or am I simply in the wrong place? I don't think I am.'

Mar Ten seemed worried for a moment. 'We used infinity-rated components for this job, so Murphy's Law shouldn't apply here.' He tapped his front teeth reflectively. 'I suppose I ought to go by the book and carry out all the standard test procedures, but that would take all night and it's getting cold. So I'd advise you to do what any sensible person would. Give the so-and-so a good jolt. About five megavolts at a tenth of an ampere. If that doesn't shift it, nothing will.'

Qenet nodded. She put her hands up again, braced herself and switched on. Everything seemed to happen at once: a flare of lightning shot from her fingers and blasted into the hillside a few yards in front of her. The ground heaved and the onlookers staggered back as a shock wave, closely followed by a cloud of steamy spray, engulfed them. 'Bingo!' exclaimed Mar Ten.

A circular patch of ground had elevated itself like some monstrous bath-plug and was hovering about ten feet above their heads. Clumps of grass and pieces of chalk showered down from its ragged edge. Qenet could be seen silhouetted against the faintly illuminated mouth of a tunnel leading into the hill. Even she appeared slightly taken aback by the dramatic success of her unorthodox method of entry. Mar Ten ran forward and grabbed Rexy by one of his arms. 'We'd better get in quick. Someone may have seen your ladyship's performance and be coming to investigate. We'll be down where the car's parked at ten tomorrow morning,' he shouted over his shoulder as he led the dinosaur into the opening. 'Thanks for the ride. Seeya.' Almost at once, with a subdued 'whoosh', the entry disc settled in place behind them. Josie, Qenet and Ben were left standing alone in the chilly dusk. Together they retraced their footsteps back to the car. It had been a long day and they were all very tired.

DAY SEVEN

The next morning, with Ben at the wheel, they took the car back to the overgrown and deserted petrol station by Silbury Hill. As Ben cautiously nosed the car into the old forecourt Mar Ten materialised from behind a clump of gorse bushes. ''Morning all,' he called, opening the driver's door and peering inquisitively at the controls. Rexy's back there somewhere chasing rabbits. Hunting small mammals comes naturally to dinosaurs – that's why your early ancestors never had a chance to evolve into larger forms during the Cretaceous. I wonder if rabbits taste as good as multituberculate raccoons – to a dinosaur, I mean. They're very finicky eaters, you know.'

He was interrupted by a great noise of crashing and snapping in the undergrowth behind him, and, a moment later, T. Rexy himself emerged. He stopped dead on seeing the others and cocked his head to one side as though trying to recollect half-faded images of the previous day's adventure. Then his eyes lit up and he galloped over, snuffling and demanding attention.

Qenet, after giving the dinosaur a rather perfunctory pat or two, glanced meaningly at the road. Three articulated lorries were clanking past in convoy. 'If anyone claps eyes on your pet,' she began to Mar Ten, 'we'll have a Loch Ness situation on our hands. Can we go and talk somewhere a little less obvious? Life here is complicated enough as it is!' She sighed. The elf was unabashed. With a sweeping bow he indicated a large petrol storage manhole cover set in the grass beside a battered red petrol pump some distance away in the direction of Silbury Hill. 'My new back door,' he announced with a mock pride which set Josie giggling. 'Pray enter my 'umble 'ome, gentles all.'

He ushered them on to the rusty cast-iron cover and quickly scanned the road to make sure it was clear. The rigid and ungiving surface of the metal dissolved around them and they sank gently through the cover. It was just like sand going through a sieve, Ben reflected, as the surface rose steadily up to his chest, his chin and his mouth. The interface was clearly visible as it passed his eyes. Then they were standing on what was immediately recognisable as another force-field tunnel. 'Luckily there was a standard emergency tool-kit in the old control chamber,' explained Mar Ten

as he led them forward, 'and there's quite a pile of spare compo
nents left over from the original installation.'

Their presence must have actuated the light, for as they ad
vanced the space ahead of them lit up, while behind them th
tunnel relapsed into darkness. The control chamber of Silbur
Hill, when they reached it, was something of a let-down. As Ma
Ten had said, the transfer equipment had been ripped out at som
distant time in the past, leaving a sphere about twenty feet in
radius which was virtually empty apart from an assortment o
sarsen and quartzite stones of various shapes and sizes scattere
randomly over the inner surface. A number of what appeared to b
fastening bolts and brackets projected at intervals from the con
tinuous wall, floor and ceiling and there was a certain amount o
force-field furniture, perceptible by its faint misty light. The air
however, was warm and fresh.

At the apex of what (viewed from the entrance) appeared to b
the roof was another tunnel which rose like a chimney-shaf
towards the top of the hill. Once again Josie and Ben experienced
moment of panic-like dizziness as the party began to traverse the
gravity-stabilised surface of the chamber. Then, as their sense
adjusted and they moved forwards, the vertical shaft slowl
appeared to swing into a horizontal plane. It seemed quite level a
they entered it and, after about twenty yards or so, curved gentl
downwards into another room, slightly larger than the contro
chamber, but disc-shaped with a gravity-positive floor and wall
about ten feet high.

Mar Ten brought out his silver control panel and pressed it. Th
circular wall grew lighter then cleared to a tinted transparency
Ahead of them, across the valley, was the familiar hump of the lon
barrow, now, of course, surrounded by the Ministry's fence. Belov
ran the road from Marlborough to Beckhampton. Between lay the
river and the bright green of Swallowhead Springs. They wer
looking out from the top of Silbury Hill.

'It's a one-way visual system, of course,' said Mar Ten. 'The Hil
is still effectively camouflaged from outside. We've got 360-degre
vision. See, there's Snid's gang up at the Sanctuary.' They al
crowded over to the left where, beyond the ploughed edge of Wader
Hill, they could see the road climbing up past the Kennett village
to the Overton ridge. A number of vehicles were parked at the to
just beside the Ridgeway crossing. Mar Ten pressed his contro
panel and zoomed in on the scene. Now the watchers in Silbury
could make out two of Snid's green Range Rovers, each marke
with the black and red clawed hand of Krasnog. Parked in lin
with them was a grey Ministry of Ancient Monuments van. A high

100

wall of wooden panels had been erected around the Sanctuary site itself. It was guarded by uniformed attendants.

Qenet was the first to speak. 'We must make some decisions – quickly. Snid's bound to be worried by my presence in this sector, so he'll be going flat out to force his way through the time lock. We *must* find out exactly what he's planning to do.' She turned to Mar Ten. 'Can you bug his communications network?'

Mar Ten kept his gaze fixed speculatively on Overton Hill. 'You reckon his outfit is based at Salisbury University with stations here, at Ot Moor and on one of the OHAG oil-rigs in the North Sea. I've done some preliminary work on the co-ordinates you gave me. Look.' He adjusted his control panel and a large illuminated map of the British Isles and western Scandinavia replaced the view outside. 'We're *here*,' said Mar Ten, and a green dot appeared. 'Salisbury's *here*' – another dot. 'the air base and the OHAG field are up around there.' Two more dots winked on, one of them a long way to the north. 'They'll communicate on closed electromagnetic beams of some sort. That means we'll need a mobile detector unit and a decoder. I can probably rig up something that'll do the job from the odds and ends we've got here.' He almost seemed to be talking to himself. 'Now, let's look at the network pattern.'

Red lines appeared and joined up the dots on the map. 'Well, what do you know?' Mar Ten exclaimed, raising his voice. 'Snid and Krasnog are working along a single-beam axis – Salisbury, Ot Moor and the OHAG field are on one straight line. That means they'll be using a linear contour beam, which should make our job much easier. To fix an interception co-ordinate all we've got to do is find the highest point along the axis.'

He pressed the control panel again and a flashing blue dot appeared on the red line connecting the positions of Salisbury and the OHAG rig. Mar Ten zeroed in on the area around the dot; the large-scale outline dissolved and in its place appeared a detailed map. The red line and the flashing pinpoint remained. There were names on the map, but both the humans recognised the area without even reading them. So did Qenet, but Josie was the first to speak:

'That's the Ridgeway, isn't it? Somewhere on the Downs between Wayland's Smithy and White Horse Hill?'

The elf nodded. 'We'll tap his communications beam most easily there. Is the Ridgeway as rough and bumpy as it used to be in prehistoric times?' he asked. Ben nodded. 'It's pretty rugged up there, but they can get Land Rovers and trials motorbikes along it without too much trouble. I don't know if our car will make it, though, even with the hydropneumatics on the rough-ride setting.'

101

Mar Ten grinned. 'Ah, yes, the orange *siabur charput*. With your permission I'd like to have a closer look at that intriguing piece of improbable mechanism. Perhaps we can tune it up a little. And its radio too. With any luck we should be able to make a passable mobile interception unit from it.'

'That would be a relief,' interrupted Qenet. 'If only we can eavesdrop on Snid and his odious playmates we'll stand some chance of being a step or two ahead of him – not behind, as we are at the moment. You two' – she nodded at Mar Ten and Ben – 'had better shove off and get the car organised. We'll stay up here and see what we can detect on the visual screens. Snid's only using light vehicles at the moment, so he can't have installed much in the way of laser equipment up at the Sanctuary yet.'

Ben and the elf made their way back to the manhole. 'Her ladyship's getting into her stride now,' commented the latter companionably. 'Notice how she's slinging her orders around? Just like Boudicca, Cartimandua, Maeve and the rest of those Celtic warrior queens. Now *they* were a bunch of real terrors. Brains, beauty and brawn. You couldn't see the Romans for dust unless they had a three-to-one superiority in men and even then you could hear their knees knocking. Qenet was really shattered when Boudicca came to a sticky end; I reckon she came as near to breaking the Statute of Limitations then as she ever has before or since. Normally she's a bit on the soft side, as goddesses go, but she can be a real handful when she's roused, though don't tell her I told you so.' They reached the manhole and rose to the surface. 'There's no one around,' said Mar Ten. 'Otherwise the lift wouldn't have operated. Now, Ben, show me this car of yours.'

Mar Ten gave the Citroën a thorough going-over; the ignition and carburettor assemblies particularly interested him. Next he sat himself in the driver's seat, switched on the radio and ran the tuner along each of the wavebands in turn. Finally he reopened the bonnet and prodded around at the front suspension units and the hydropneumatic accumulator. As he examined each component he fired a series of questions about its function at Ben. 'Well,' he said eventually, 'I'd like to build situation analysis and response circuits into the ignition and carburation systems; at the moment there's a crude advance/retard control over the timing mechanism and virtually no flexibility at all in the carburettor. I can't do much for your radio – it's too primitive, I'm afraid, but I reckon I can improvise a twelve-volt closed-beam decoder and build it into the chassis. And I think the suspension can be beefed up without blowing any of the seals. Then we'll be able to keep an eye on the

102

White Horse section of the Ridgeway. Is it O.K. by you if I go ahead?'

Ben nodded more or less automatically but nevertheless felt rather apprehensive as, with obvious enthusiasm, Mar Ten took a ratchet and leant over into the engine compartment. 'Catch,' he called out after a few minutes, tossing out a selection of nuts, bolts and washers. Ben complied. Next came the distributor and, after what seemed to be a sharp tussle, the carburettor. 'They don't half pack the bits and pieces close together in these engines,' muttered Mar Ten. By now his neat appearance was somewhat tarnished: his shirt had long streaks of grease across the chest and sleeves, while his trousers were marked with lines of oil where he had unconsciously wiped his hands. There was a blob of grease on his face and his hair had taken on a green tinge where some hydraulic fluid had spurted on to it.

Laden with an assortment of mechanical and electrical components, they returned to the old control chamber under the hill, to be greeted effusively by Rexy, who joined Ben in watching as Mar Ten placed the bits and pieces on one of the force-field supports and began to sort through some of the smaller chunks of sarsen rock that littered the floor. At length he picked one up and handed it to Ben. 'Can you just hold this for a minute or so?' he asked. 'And while you're doing so try to imagine that you're driving the car fast along a difficult road.'

Ben complied. He was by now used to the strange requests of his Otherworld acquaintances; he remembered the hair-raising episode on Wroughton Hill and pretended that he was driving over the same length of road. Almost at once the section of the force-field around the car's distributor began to radiate a bright green light. Mar Ten was pleased. 'Good; you've established empathy at the first go. Now try this piece.' The carburettor took rather longer to match. Only after Mar Ten had tried several other stone fragments did they obtain a response.

'What I'm trying to do,' he explained, 'is to relate your thoughts to the car, so that if you want maximum speed or minimum fuel consumption or whatever, the car itself will try to co-operate. The natural circuits inside these stones are able to pick up your thought patterns, so what I've got to do now is build a couple of electrical relays to pass on your wishes to the ignition and fuel control systems of the car.'

Mar Ten's explanation was interrupted by the appearance of Qenet and Josie, who had materialised at the shaft entrance and were now walking round the curved wall of the control chamber to where the others were standing. 'Something's happened up at the

103

Sanctuary,' announced Josie. 'A massive articulated lorry has just arrived at the lay-by there. Qenet and I thought we'd wander over and chat up some of the workmen to find out what's going on. Want to come?'

Ben glanced at Mar Ten, who nodded. 'I won't be needing you for an hour or so. By then I should have fitted up the car; I might have to make a few fine adjustments later when you're driving but you can go away in the meantime. Make sure that animal doesn't get out,' he called after them as Rexy, sensing the chance of a walk in the sun, started to follow. The dinosaur sat looking reproachfully as they rose through the manhole exit and made their way on to the main road.

Turning left, they tramped along the grass verge towards Overton Hill. Ten minutes or so later they were near enough to the ridge to see quite clearly the newly arrived lorry, which had been squeezed into the lay-by there. One of the Range Rovers had been moved to make room for it and was now parked beside the road a few yards down the hill. Seven or eight men were standing around the closed tailgate, apparently waiting for something to happen. Charlie and his companion – the two workmen from the long barrow – were there. 'Hi there, beautiful,' he called out as soon as he saw Qenet. 'Feeling better today?' He came over towards them.

Qenet smiled encouragingly. 'All the better for seeing you,' she replied. 'What's all the fuss about?' she jerked her head at the lorry. 'Have your Ministry friends brought along a plastic replica of Stonehenge for the tourist trade?' Charlie grinned. 'No – it's more equipment up from Salisbury. They're going to unload it any minute. Stick around and you can watch.'

The driver had left his cab and now he came round to the back. Looking rather self-conscious, he pressed the tailgate release and, with a hiss of compressed air, the door slowly descended to form an unloading ramp. Just inside the load compartment stood a yellow and black fork-lift truck. The driver got in, started it and carefully backed down. Lashed to the loading platform was a gun-like object. Black-boxed and trolley-mounted, it carried the familiar legend: 'Laser; ruby; pulsed; nominal capacity 1 terawatt (10^{12} watts). Extreme danger to objects within total line-of-sight range in Normal Atmospheric Conditions. For Experimental Use Only.' A festoon of coaxial cables was hooked around it and fastened down with heavy tape. It was one of the laser cannon which Ben and Josie had last seen in the basement of Snid's headquarters at Salisbury University.

The fork-lift truck drove off and entered the Sanctuary enclosure. A few minutes later it re-emerged, trundled up the ramp into the lorry and emerged carrying the computer for the laser.

By now there was a small crowd around the site: tourists from Avebury; one or two Ridgeway hikers, lorry drivers from the nearby café and a number of schoolchildren. Everyone stood around for a few minutes wondering what was going to happen next. Then the whine of the fork-lift truck's motor started again and it drove back to the lay-by. The computer had been unloaded and balanced on the platform was the leather-clothed figure of Krasnog, his long red hair catching the wind and half covering his face as he directed the driver to manœuvre his vehicle into the space between the Ministry van and the nearest Range Rover. The mere appearance of Krasnog seemed to subdue the spirits of the onlookers. Charlie and the other workmen half stiffened to attention as his piercing blue eyes swept across the crowd. Josie and Ben felt their stomachs turn over as his glance rested briefly on them. Qenet, with her usual catlike reactions, had already disappeared behind them, ostensibly stooping to adjust a shoe.

'Get in there, you, you, you and you,' shouted Krasnog, pointing to four of the workmen. He waved them up into the lorry. 'Bring out the flat-top trolley. Place it there.' He indicated the ground at the foot of the ramp. 'Now fetch the large crate. Take care, you. . . .' He lapsed into a bout of proto-Celtic swear-words. The four men, staggering under the weight of a large wooden box, descended the ramp. As they emerged from the lorry the stencilled words 'University of Salisbury, Department of Physics' came into view and, underneath them, the further description 'Experimental M.H.D. plasma converter. Handle with extreme caution. Unit (1) of 3 units.'

As soon as the men had deposited the crate on the trolley Krasnog beckoned to the fork-lift driver. The latter backed his truck over, hitched it to the trolley and drove off once again into the enclosure. This procedure was repeated with the second and third units of the converter. Krasnog supervised the work, his temper growing shorter as time passed. His bullying manner, with its hints of scarcely suppressed violence, unnerved the workmen and caused them to take an unnecessarily long time over the job. But at last the lorry was empty, whereupon Krasnog seized the driver and practically threw him behind the wheel. The engine spluttered to life and the vehicle drew out into the road and moved off towards Bath.

Comparative peace returned to the site for perhaps a quarter of an hour; and then, to the accompaniment of a continuous screaming roar, the reason for Krasnog's anxiety to unload the lorry as quickly as possible became apparent. A huge crawler truck, its cab-top lights flashing, slowly ascended the hill and drew into the lay-by. Under the guidance of Krasnog it mounted the kerb, crunched across the verge and entered the field beside the Sanctuary. Then it slewed off the track and stopped about thirty yards from a round barrow which stood beside the line of the Ridgeway. The pitch of the diesel engine changed as the hydraulic stands of the rear platform engaged and descended to anchor it to the earth. The whole assembly ponderously raised itself about five feet from the ground. Then the driver cut the engine and jumped down beside Krasnog. The two of them at once began talking as a group of the onlookers, Josie and Ben among them, followed the tracks of the crawler into the field in order to have a better look at the enormous vehicle.

On first inspection it appeared to be a self-propelled transporter – not unlike an enlarged version of the tank carriers that from time to time growled along the roads to and from the military training areas on the Plain. But the gaudy red-and-white striped paintwork proclaimed that it was a civil vehicle. Its canvas-covered load was about forty feet long and wedged-shaped, with the sharp end projecting several feet beyond the rear wheels. It was all very mystifying, but not for long. Their conversation finished, Krasnog and the driver separated. Krasnog yelled to the workmen, who began to unlash the canvas. At the same time the engine started up again. The sharp rear end of the load began to swing upwards in an arc. Soon it had elevated itself fully to present an elongated A profile. The engine stopped, the covers fell away and there, in the middle of a Wiltshire field, towered the unmistakable outline of an oil derrick. Vertical red fluorescent letters down its side spelt out the acronym OHAG.

Suddenly everything made sense. Snid, Krasnog and their allies must have decided to abandon their experiment with the fusion torus. Instead they were going to use a hydrogen bomb to initiate the laser pulse which would open up the Transfer Station at West Kennett. The oil drill was there to excavate the shaft for the bomb itself. Soon the laser, its computer and the M.H.D. converter would be linked and lined up on the long barrow across the valley. Somewhere in the future something – a doomsday weapon perhaps – was already waiting to come through the time gate. All Snid needed now was the bomb; without that he could do nothing How deep down, wondered Ben, did you have to bury a tactical nuclear weapon in order to use its exploding plasma? And how long would it take the OHAG drill to bore that far? As though in answer to his unspoken question the great diesel motor started once more. It revved up and then settled down to a steady roar. The derrick gave a shudder as the drilling gear ground into action. They were wasting no time. The last phase of Snid's plan was about to begin.

It was in a subdued frame of mind that Qenet, Josie and Ben walked back along the A 4 road to Silbury Hill. The prospect of Snid exploding a nuclear bomb (albeit a buried one) in the neighbourhood was not exactly a cheering one. The only redeeming feature of the situation was the fact that his plans now depended entirely upon obtaining a weapon, and hydrogen bombs, even low-yield ones, were not a commodity to be bought at the local army surplus store. So perhaps the security precautions of the United States Air Force would yet bring all Snid's schemes to nothing.

'I suppose they couldn't have swiped an H-bomb on the quiet?' It was Josie who voiced a thought common to all of them. 'Wouldn't a theft like that be reported at once?' 'Not if they slapped a D-notice on it; that would prevent the papers from mentioning it,' replied Ben. They continued in silence for a few minutes. As they reached the little bridge where the Kennet ran under the road, the goddess stopped and turned towards her left, where the river ran in a wide right-angled bend past Swallowhead Springs. 'You know,' she said, 'Mar Ten was right. If that mind-poisoned bogle really does manage to steal a bomb, I'm inclined to think there's only one thing for me – us – to do.' They waited. 'We really ought to call in the Furies. This sector's on Alecto's beat. She's not bad, for a Fury anyway. If Finky Snid and Krasnog start letting off their fireworks up at the Sanctuary I'll certainly be asked why I haven't sent out a request for intervention.' She sighed in her best poor-little-girl way. 'But what a confession of failure! Five thousand years of looking after my area without any trouble at all and now this! I'll pay back those two *mucs* if it's the last thing I do. Anyway, I'm going to wait until the last possible moment before screaming for help. If the worst comes to the worst I'll fry them up with a blast of the old terapower and damn the consequences.' The thought seemed to cheer her considerably.

Mar Ten, more grease-stained than before, emerged from the car as the party approached. He, at least, seemed to be in high spirits. 'All finished,' he called out. The car looked much the same: the radio aerial had certainly been modified – the antenna was more sturdy than before and what appeared to be a small aluminium dish had been clipped to the top of it. But otherwise there were no external signs of alteration.

Undeterred by the gloom of the others, the elf explained what he had been doing: 'I've rigged up a communications receiver in the right-hand glove-box.' He pointed to a plain black fascia board in which were set six pressure plates. 'I think it should be adequate for our purpose.' He pressed plates labelled 'Air' and 'Track'. A servo motor hummed somewhere behind the dashboard and the dish antenna began to rotate. The radio picked up a faint signal which rapidly strengthened as the antenna locked on to its source: 'Gazelle Red Three to Chieftain Leader Range Ten monitor.' There was a background beat of helicopter rotors. 'Your group's last salvo was 450, repeat 450 metres off target. You only just missed the officers' mess. For Pete's sake do better next time. Out.' 'Gunnery practice on the Plain.' said Mar Ten. He pressed a third plate: 'Alpha Orange Three, Alpha Orange Three,' called a new voice. 'Please proceed to M 4 intersection 14 where an articulated lorry has shed its load of scrap iron across eastbound access road.'

Mar Ten switched off. 'It's got a range of about two thousand miles,' he added. 'For long range reception you have to set the approximate co-ordinates on the digital counter here. I've also built in a decoder for closed beams and a mix facility so that we can listen to several transmissions at once. The only likely danger, as far as I can see, is that if they're operating on a really tight beam it might just be possible to detect us tapping it. Now, Ben, change places with me and let's test the engine.'

He was about to turn the ignition key when Qenet placed a hand on his shoulder and explained the situation to him. 'So the sooner you can get some information about how Finky and Krasnog plan to hijack that nuclear bomb the better,' she concluded. 'Is the car ready to drive up to the Ridgeway at once?'

Forty minutes later the Citroën bumped off the Shrivenham–Newbury road on to the uneven surface of the ancient trackway. Ben was driving; Mar Ten sat beside him and Rexy the dinosaur was sprawled on the rear seat, wrapped in the blue anorak. Qenet had been doubtful, to say the least, about allowing the tyrannosaur to accompany the other two but Mar Ten had insisted. So throughout the journey he had sat halfway round in his seat with a hand on Rexy's head ready to push the animal out of sight at the approach of any oncoming vehicle. Nothing overtook them; the effectiveness of the elf's engineering made the orange demon chariot the fastest car on the road. At first Ben had not noticed much difference in its performance except that the noise level was lower. When they had stopped in Marlborough to buy some fish and chips for lunch he had discovered that he could move off in top gear without difficulty. Nor did he have to change down for hills – even the steep climb up from Ashbury to the Ridgeway had been done in top. But what had become apparent on the relatively short drive up from Silbury was that the car was almost anticipating his intentions. The steering and braking remained entirely manual but in other respects the car seemed to have developed an uncanny ability to interpret his wishes and to respond to them automatically.

The Ridgeway was deserted. Ben shifted the suspension control to cope with its rutted surface, dried hard by the sunshine of the previous few days. Mar Ten clipped on the dish antenna and pressed the 'Track' and 'Decode' plates of the receiver. Rexy sat up and poked his long nose out of the offside rear window, snuffling at the as yet unfamiliar scents of the Quaternary world.

The receiver remained silent as the Citroën edged slowly forwards. On the left there appeared the jagged sarsen facade of Wayland's Smithy long barrow. The ridgeway was just beginning to widen out on its approach to the access road when a precise, rather flat voice said, '. . . fifty feet down already . . .'. 'Finky,' whispered Mar Ten, and Ben jammed the brakes on, though not before the transmission had faded. He reversed for a few yards. '. . . no perceptible wear on the drill,' continued Snid's voice, 'so we should be able to complete the detonation chamber within twenty-four hours. Negative signals only from Ot Moor. How long do you need to complete the installation of your CO_2 laser?'

An American voice came on the air. 'Final checks almost complete. Generator, radar and ranging computer connected up and in phase. Give us thirty minutes and we'll be ready to act on your signal. Recovery submarine has been swung out for immediate lowering. Confirm that interception during daylight is imperative. Cannot plot impact point accurately enough on radar; visual sighting essential for rapid recovery. Sub will deliver firework to consignment location during hours of darkness. Out.'

The transmitter on the oil-rig was switched off. The radio beam fell silent except for an intermittent click and some unidentifiable howling sounds in the background. The eavesdroppers in the car waited, despite growing signs of restiveness on the part of Rexy. After about fifteen minutes the howling began a crescendo and resolved itself into the unmistakable racket of an F111 engine. 'That must be Snid's sensor transmitting from Ot Moor air base,' said Ben. Mar Ten nodded. The metronome-like clicking continued as the plane took off, passed over the monitor and receded into the distance. Mar Ten leant forward and pressed the 'Track' and 'Air' plates of the radio. At once another American voice came through. This time it was the pilot of the F111 reporting his bearing to the control tower. The air traffic officer confirmed that he was on course and then this conversation, too, finished.

Ben felt a weight on his left shoulder. He glanced sideways and saw Rexy's snout resting upon it. The dinosaur nudged him towards the door. Ben looked up and down the track; it still seemed deserted. He turned inquiringly to Mar Ten. 'That's O.K.,' said the latter. 'You take Rexy for a walk. I'll stay here and monitor the air-base traffic. My guess is that nothing will happen today. We'll simply have to come up here each day until interception is made and an F111 brought down. Then things will start happening quickly enough!'

Ben swung his door open. Rexy waited for him to open the tailgate and, shedding his anorak, stepped sedately on to the Ridgeway. He snuffled around for a few moments and then bounded off up the track towards Wayland's Smithy. As soon as he reached the elderberry hedge he veered off into the trees and, much to Ben's relief, vanished from sight. Crashes from the undergrowth indicated his presence somewhere in the background. After about ten minutes the dinosaur emerged. He had a smug expression and was licking his lips. Ben wondered rather anxiously what it was he had been hunting. Together they walked towards the long barrow. Rexy surveyed the gate at the entrance with puzzlement. Then, with a challenging snort, he advanced up to it and sprang, apparently without undue effort, clean over the barrier. He landed softly on the far side, his powerful hind legs acting as efficient shock-absorbers. Ben followed. Rexy repeated his jack-in-the-box performance at the second gate and together the incongruous pair explored the ancient monument.

It was dusk when they returned to the car. Mar Ten had nothing further to report: the steady clicking of the radiation counter indicated that no nuclear weapons had left the base at Ot Moor. Soon it would be too dark for the watchers on the oil-rig to go into action. With a feeling of relief Ben eased the car over the remaining few yards of track to the road and made for Silbury and home.

It was, of course, the fifth of November, and a few early rockets began to arc up into the sky as they descended from the Ridgeway into the vale below and one or two bonfires winked on in otherwise invisible villages. That evening, as Josie, Ben and Qenet watched the local charity firework display, the mind of each constantly returned to the much more spectacular show which their enemies were currently preparing not far away on Overton Hill.

110

DAY EIGHT

Early next morning Ben was back on the Ridgeway. This time he had Qenet as companion, for the goddess had insisted that she should take a more active part in the proceedings than just sit inside Silbury Hill helplessly watching the sinister preparations of Snid and Krasnog. Mar Ten had agreed with reluctance; not that he had much choice – Qenet's mixture of winsome cajolery and queenly determination was irresistible. He had accepted the situation good-humouredly enough and wandered off to tinker with the viewing systems inside the hill. Rexy, on the other hand, was obviously determined to have another day out on the Ridgeway and had insinuated himself into the car at an early stage of the proceedings.

The three of them were parked as unobtrusively as possible on the verge of the track a couple of hundred yards to the east of Wayland's Smithy. Ahead of them the dusty white line of the Ridgeway dipped and then rose to meet the imposing bulk of the Iron Age hill-fort on White Horse Hill. Already they could discern the elongated outlines of a few people on the ramparts, but their section of the ancient road was as deserted as it had been on the previous day.

The closed-beam transmissions had little to reveal. The monitor at Ot Moor was clicking regularly and from time to time the sound of an F111 taking off or landing could be heard. But there was no exchange of information between Snid's headquarters at Salisbury and the laser installation on the OHAG oil-rig in the North Sea.

Ben, exhilarated by his new mastery over the performance of the car, was feeling less worried than at any time since Qenet's surprise arrival in the twentieth century. The goddess herself, Mar Ten, Josie, Rexy and he all seemed to be getting on fine together. The slight strains of the first few days had vanished. He wondered if there really was anything in all that talk about symbiosis. Anyway, the mere presence of Qenet beside him in the car was enough to lend a certain glamour and attraction to the day's work. Ben wished that some of his school acquaintances could by chance stroll past and see them together. It would do wonders for his status.

111

Qenet herself, by contrast, was ill at ease. The enormity of Snid's intended action and its possible consequences continued to worry her. There remained in her mind a deep sense of guilt that her preference for the pre-Roman era had allowed her so to neglect the land assigned to her that such a plot could be hatched at its very core, the Avebury–Silbury–Sanctuary triangle. Her intuition, moreover, told her that something was going to happen very soon, and that it wasn't going to be at all nice.

'Do you mind if I take a look at Wayland's Smithy, Ben?' she asked. 'It used originally to be a Series I Transfer Station, but it was completely dismantled when the circles took over. I haven't seen what the last four thousand years have done to it. I won't be long. Coming, Rexy?'

The dinosaur blinked a wary eye. He, too, seemed rather subdued this morning. The only move he made was to clamber into Qenet's front seat as soon as she had vacated it and then lean against Ben, listening with his head tilted to the ticking of the monitor's radiation counter. Qenet closed the door, first gently flicking Rexy's tail out of the way, and began to walk back along the track. Soon she was out of sight between the hedges. Ben and Rexy relapsed into their respective daydreams.

It was Qenet's cry of alarm that brought Ben back to his senses. He turned round in time to see her appear along the Ridgeway track behind him. She had hitched her green and gold dress up to her knees and was running towards the car. Almost at the same instant his attention was diverted by a movement even further up the track. A vehicle careered into sight; it was a Range Rover, painted green. Attached to its aerial was a dish antenna like the one on the Citroën and on its door Ben could just about make out the hooked-claw sign.

Without thinking Ben started the car and shoved it into reverse. Within a few seconds Qenet had drawn level, opened a rear door and jumped in. Ben changed into first gear and accelerated. 'It's Krasnog,' gasped Qenet. 'He recognised me and tried to run me down. Somehow or other they must have detected us picking up their transmissions.'

By now their car, with the Range Rover about twenty-five yards behind, had reached the access road to Wayland's Smithy. Ben turned to the left, down the steepening slope which ran towards the Port Way road at the foot of the chalk downs. He remembered the hatred in Krasnog's voice at Salisbury and shivered. 'Why didn't you blast him?' he shouted above the noise of the car. 'He's only human.' Qenet tossed her head, 'And that's why,' she shouted back. 'Immortals can only fight immortals. I thought I'd told you that.

112

It's part of the Statute. If anyone's going to spike Krasnog it's got to be you – or Josie. That's what symbiosis is all about.'

Ben, wrestling with the wheel and pedals of the bouncing Citroën, felt as though the sky had fallen in on him. The very *thought* of Krasnog turned his knees to jelly. The prospect of a duel with him was utterly terrifying. Then Qenet's elbow nudged his shoulder. He spared a sideways glance at her as she leaned forward against the back of Rexy's seat. She winked and patted the dinosaur's head. 'But we'll do all we can to help Ben, won't we, Rexy?' she added. He felt a little better.

The car had almost reached the Port Way. They seemed to have gained a little on the Range Rover. Ben would have to make his mind up whether to turn left to Ashbury, right towards Uffington or to carry directly on down into the Vale of the White Horse. He knew that on a straight road the heavily engined Range Rover would stand a good chance of overtaking the Citroën. On the other hand the improved suspension and responsiveness of the smaller car should have made it more manoeuvrable on winding roads. Ben took a deep breath and pulled the steering-wheel clockwise. The demon chariot lurched, skidded slightly and then picked up speed round the tight curves of the road that led them along below the deep coombs and towering mass of White Horse Hill. Krasnog began to lose yet more ground; from time to time he was out of sight round corners. Ben momentarily experienced a warm tremor of confidence. No more than that, but at least it was something.

Now there was another decision to take. There was a second crossroads ahead: left for Uffington, straight on for Wantage, or a sharp upward incline to the right. This, Ben knew, was the one-way approach road to the great prehistoric White Horse itself; one-way because the narrow lane climbed steeply through the gap between White Horse Hill and Dragon Hill and then swung precariously round the ravine-like escarpment at the top of the coomb. The idea of driving at speed along the dizzy sweep of track five hundred feet above the valley floor was unnerving – but less so than that of being rammed off the road by the bumpers of Krasnog's Range Rover. So sharp right it was. Down into second gear and up between the two hills.

Ben considered the geography of the place: the lane, he remembered, went up across the escarpment to the car park by the old hill-fort. Dragon Hill, in shape at least resembling a small version of Silbury, was on his right. Dimly he recalled how he and Josie had once watched some motor-cyclists scrambling their bikes up and round it and in a flash he knew what to do. Before Krasnog could come round the bend he would try to steer the car off the road and, trusting to Mar Ten's improved suspension, swing it over the top and then down behind Dragon Hill. There they would be out of sight from the road and with any luck Krasnog would carry straight on until he reached the summit. After that, the one-way system would carry him on until he reached the exit road on the other side.

The Citroën groaned and lurched as Ben swerved off the road; the car tilted alarmingly as it negotiated the footpath up to the bare summit of the mound. Then with a crash it bucketed over the flat top and pitched down the far side. Ben, trembling, eased it round in a tight circle and brought its nose up towards the top. As he pulled on the handbrake he became aware once again of Rexy's presence next to him. The animal was hanging on to the dashboard with his diminutive hands, an expression of deep enjoyment on his face. Even as Ben suppressed a rather panicky laugh, the dinosaur turned his grinning jaws towards him as though asking for more.

Qenet, meanwhile, had already jumped out; she climbed up the side of Dragon Hill and peered cautiously over the top. She turned round at once, giving the thumbs-up sign. Evidently Krasnog had driven past, unaware that he was no longer pursuing his quarry. Pausing to unclip the dish antenna, Qenet re-entered the car and Ben slipped the clutch to ease it forward up the slope. The road was clear and within seconds they were back on it, driving slowly to allow Krasnog to increase his lead.

As they entered the dangerous stretch above the near-vertical back slope up the coomb Ben took the car over to the left, as far as possible from the insubstantial wooden fencing that overhung the drop below. Behind him, Qenet suddenly stiffened and then nudged him. 'There's something ahead. I can sense it. Just round the next corner. And it's coming towards us. Look out!'

Ben eased the accelerator pedal back and drew in even further to the side. Then, round the curve ahead, came Krasnog's Range Rover. Not finding them at the top, and suspecting that they had tricked him somehow, he had decided to retrace his route, ignoring the large one-way warning signs by the car park.

A surge of terror overwhelmed Ben. Krasnog's vehicle seemed so massive as it bore down upon them. He considered going into reverse and backing downhill but knew it would be no use. He could see Krasnog now, a grin of malice and glee on his face, as the Range Rover accelerated down towards them.

Once again something clicked at the back of Ben's mind. Everything seemed to come vividly into focus and go into a kind of slow motion. A single glance at the Range Rover, the road before him and the ravine to the right and his mind was made up. There was only one thing he could do: steer his nearside wheels as far up the bank as possible and drive the Citroën like a wedge between Krasnog and the cliff-edge side of the road. If he could do that, the two cars would come abreast with Krasnog's on the outside. In that position it couldn't possibly keep all four wheels on the track – there simply wasn't room.

Rexy was by now looking mildly excited: he craned forward, his snout hard against the windscreen, bared his teeth, and *roared*. That roar was a sound from a nightmare; there was something blood-freezingly primeval about it. Possibly Krasnog heard it. At all events his eyes shifted from Ben to the dinosaur. Slowly, or so it seemed, his expression of triumph changed to one of horror and dread. His mouth opened; perhaps he screamed. Then everything seemed to happen at once. The Range Rover sheered outwards into the middle of the lane and the Citroën, now canted over at about forty-five degrees, clanged into its offside wing. There was a crunch of metal and a rending clatter as a sizeable chunk of the Range Rover's aluminium mudguard wrapped itself round the Citroën's front wheel. Over his shoulder Ben caught a glimpse of the other vehicle slewing through the roadside fence. It seemed for a moment to hang in the air and then it was gone.

Ben brought the car to a stop just in time to see the Range Rover somersault – it must have been for the second time – before hitting the bottom of the coomb. It lay there motionless and then, with a faint 'whoosh', its petrol tank ignited and a column of smoke began to drift upwards. With mingled relief and disappointment he made out a sprawled figure some distance from the flaming wreck. Krasnog had either jumped out or been thrown clear of his doomed vehicle.

Normality returned. Ben became aware that Qenet, her arms around his neck, was executing a cramped but triumphant war dance behind him. Rexy, for his part, was trying to get his teeth to the door-catch, evidently keen to escape and bring his encounter with Krasnog to a final conclusion. Luckily he was pretty well invisible in that position, from a distance at any rate. For round the corner at the top of the ascent came a knot of figures, led by a man in R.A.C. uniform carrying a first-aid box. Qenet released Ben quickly and, with characteristic presence of mind, covered Rexy with his anorak. Ben got out and walked rather shakily up the slope.

'You all right?' inquired the R.A.C. man. Ben nodded. 'Stupid git,' continued the other, nodding towards Krasnog. 'I tried to stop him going down this way but the silly bugger almost ran me over in that damn great Range Rover of his. Saw me, too. If he pulls through the cops'll do him for dangerous driving, that's for sure. You're both O.K., are you?' He cast a quick glance at Qenet. 'I've radioed for the lot – ambulance, police, fire brigade. Must go now. You stay here until you're feeling better, and then drive over to the car park. I expect the police will want to take your evidence.' He turned away and began to scramble down the slope towards Krasnog. The others followed him.

Still rather dizzy, Ben inspected the car. There was remarkably little damage. The impact must have been a slight one – just sufficient to upset the stability of the Range Rover enough to make it skid. The offside wing of the Citroën was quite badly crumpled and the bumper was bent inwards, though not sufficiently to catch the wheel. Ben tugged at the green-painted panel embedded under the wheel arch. It came away fairly easily. He was propping it up at the side of the road when the car's engine started. He started in surprise. Qenet was at the wheel. She pointed forwards and looked at him inquiringly. Ben nodded and jumped into the rear seat as the goddess inched the car forward. It seemed to move quite smoothly. As they reached the top of the climb the sound of sirens heralded the arrival of the police, followed closely by the ambulance and fire engine. Qenet drove past the hill-fort and down to the official car park. At the entrance she braked, reversed and pulled closely into the hedge that lined the exit road. She got out and opened the nearside door. 'Up, please, Rexy. It wouldn't do if the police discovered you here,' she said. 'Come and hide behind the trees.' Turning to Ben, she added, 'Give me a yell if I'm needed.' The shape under the anorak shifted and Rexy sat up, gazed around and ambled into the bushes behind Qenet.

Ben parked the car and waited. Fortunately he didn't have much time to think about the events of the previous half-hour, for within five minutes a large white police car turned into the car park and came to a halt beside the Citroën. Ben went to meet the two officers. Almost at once Qenet joined them, wearing the demure look which had worked so well previously. The policemen were friendly enough, even solicitous, right from the start. Perhaps they had been talking to the R.A.C. man. They breathalysed Ben and then recorded his and Qenet's accounts of the crash: how the Range Rover had suddenly appeared racing down the one-way track towards them; how Ben had driven up the nearside bank in order to give as much space as possible to the oncoming vehicle; and how, even so, the Range Rover's driver had collided with the Citroën, lost control and crashed through the fence into the coomb. 'He must have been drunk,' surmised one of the policemen. 'He's not badly injured, by the way. Concussion and a few scratches – they reckon

116

he'll be out for the count for a few hours. Nasty looking so-and-so.' He gave Qenet an approving look.

The police officers then checked the Citroën's tyres, steering and brakes and pronounced them to be in impeccable order. They noted their findings, hinted broadly that Ben and Qenet would have nothing to fear from the law, but would in all probability be called in due course to give evidence against Krasnog. Then they departed.

Ben still didn't feel too good. He was tired and rather sick and he remembered with something of a shock that the real reason for their presence on the downs was to monitor Snid's transmissions at the interception point near Wayland's Smithy. With a sigh he restarted the engine and backed up to Rexy's hiding-place. Qenet gave a whistle and, to the usual accompaniment of snapping branches, the dinosaur obediently bulldozed his way to the car. Within a few minutes they were back on the Ridgeway; fortunately, nothing much seemed to be happening. Qenet produced her bottle of green spirit, together with a thermos flask of coffee and a packet of sandwiches for Ben. The latter he shared with Rexy. Then, emotionally exhausted, he drifted off to sleep.

Qenet woke him. 'Something's happening over at Ot Moor,' she said, pressing the 'Air' and 'Mix' plates on the radio. They listened to the howl of jet engines from the monitor and the cross-talk between pilots and air control officers. Planes were taking off in quick succession. As each passed over the monitor the radiation counter transmitted a burst of clicks. That could only mean one thing – they were carrying their nuclear weapons. Then Snid began to speak, his voice disconcertingly clear as it came through Mar Ten's hi-fi system. 'OHAG – are you there? Red alert at air base. Activate all interception systems in fifteen minutes. You should be obtaining radar contact by then. Have ranging computer placed on stand-by to lock on target. Cut in main generator at once.'

The beam went dead. Planes were still taking off but nothing much else seemed to be happening. Ben began to doze off again. Qenet sat beside him with Rexy's snout resting on her shoulder, his eyes intent upon the loudspeaker.

A new voice broke in, brief and to the point. 'G.2, G.2, I have trouble. Total malfunction of starboard controls. Backup systems status negative repeat negative. Cannot hold height or course. Transponders activated. Am ejecting.' There was a muffled explosion and the voice, apparently unperturbed, continued. 'Escape module free; chutes open; support systems O.K. Impact imminent. Out.'

The F111 pilot had sounded almost casual as he reported his predicament. The reaction of the air controller at the base was anything but that. 'This is a Bent Spear emergency one,' he announced tensely. 'Initiate all procedures for recovery of crew and hot stores. Notify Keflavik. Scramble all air-sea rescue choppers from Vodø. Instruct *Key West* recovery ship to leave Holy Loch. Request time-of-impact computer analysis of area from Vela and Samos satellite systems.' The controller paused briefly. 'What surveillance forces have we got in the area?' he asked. 'There's an AWACS detector plane 150 miles S.S.W. of Lindesnes and hunter-killer atomic sub *Mako* on patrol 75 miles west of Skagerrak' replied another voice. 'I'm ordering them to divert to last known co-ordinates. E.T.A.s are about 20 minutes and 4 hours. The choppers from Vodø should rendezvous in 30 minutes.'

All went quiet for five or six minutes. Then the second voice cut in. 'We have computer map readout from Vela satellite: twin impacts in area 59.20.40 N, 2.30.15 E. All rescue units notified.'

Silence again, punctuated only by the regular tick of the radiation counter near the air base. Then the radio operator of the AWACS surveillance plane began transmission. 'We have picked up signal from F111 ejection module and are homing in. . . . We have visual contact now. Circling at 300 feet. Awaiting choppers.'

Within a quarter of an hour the helicopters from the Norwegian airfield at Vodø had joined the plane. One of them went straight down and, without any apparent difficulty, winched up the pilot and his crewman. It immediately began to stutter its way back to base. The other remained in the area: the co-pilot's message was less comforting. 'Have lowered passive sonar detectors,' he stated unemotionally; 'negative reception.' The base officer groaned. 'Oh *no*; is your equipment functional?' he asked. 'Equipment status A.1. functional; confirm negative, repeat negative transponder transmissions in this area,' the co-pilot replied. 'We have a Palomares situation; we've lost the bomb.' Along the closed beam from Salisbury came the sound of someone laughing. It didn't seem a pleasant sound, at least not to Ben and Qenet.

Qenet flicked the 'Off' plate in a gesture of finality. 'That's that, Snid's lot have heisted their bomb. We've got to stop him now, or else he'll make a radioactive shambles out of the whole Kennett-Avebury area. And the explosion there will only be the beginning of a dire disaster for this whole space-time sector. Oh, the humiliation of it! To be outwitted by a pestiferous half-demon like him.' She looked every inch a tragic queen from some melodramatic play. And though she smiled wanly at Ben's attempt to cheer her up on the way back to Silbury (where they duly reported the bad

118

news to the others) her black mood persisted throughout the rest of the day. There was no mention of the F111 incident in the news broadcasts that evening, though the car radio continued to intercept a stream of increasingly worried messages from the American military network. By the following morning the rest of the NATO forces had been alerted but the absence from the crash area of any alien submarines or ships was still delaying any suspicions that the plane's nuclear cargo might have been hijacked.

DAY NINE

The fine weather of the previous week was still holding but there was a chill in the air as Josie, Ben and Qenet walked across the familiar weed-grown area beside Silbury Hill and waited by the manhole cover for Mar Ten to appear.

Mar Ten didn't seem too worried by the depressed spirits of the others. 'It strikes me', he said with a smile, 'that this is really an elvish matter now. You know, it's high time that Master Snid and I sorted things out between us. All I hope is that I can clobber him half as efficiently as our friend here – he bowed bowards Ben – 'settled that unsavoury human Krasnog yesterday. Give me six or seven hours and I reckon I ought to be able to produce something that'll snarl up Finky's immediate programme – you know, the display he's got scheduled for the Sanctuary. Then perhaps your ladyship can take over and tidy up the legal and disciplinary aspects of the case afterwards.' And armed with an assortment of gleaming tools he wandered over to the car and began to hammer out the traces of the previous day's encounter with Krasnog's Range Rover.

This relaxed attitude didn't go down at all well with Qenet, who made an unladylike gesture at his back. 'It's all right for him,' she complained. 'He sees it all as a simple matter of honour between elves. Snid's behaving in a criminal way, so it's Mar Ten's duty to straighten him out. Oh, he'll do his best, I'm sure, but what about the wider implications? It's in my territory that all this is happening, you know. I'm supposed to keep an eye on what goes on here. There's the biggest concentration of Otherworld technology on this planet within the Avebury triangle – or at least there used to be. If news of what Snid's been up to leaks out my name will be mud with the Higher Authorities. Damn Snid, damn him!' In an access of exasperation she stamped her foot. Josie and Ben exchanged an uneasy glance; they hoped she wasn't going to project herself into a Mode 3 temper – things were quite bad enough without *that*. But the goddess's appearance remained stable. 'Just look at what that crazy *muc* is trying to do. One, he's perverted human agencies for his own illegal use. Two, he's planning to blast open my Transfer Station – *mine*, mark you, without so much as a by-your-leave – in order to bring in temporally anomalous technology. Three, by his own demented admission he's going to try to take this whole sector out of the continuum with force-field isolators. Talk about tearing up the Statute! There's been nothing like it for millennia. And never in my territory. Never.' She paused, and continued in a quieter voice. 'I can't let it happen, you know. If the worst comes to the worst I really will have to blast him, like I said. A few terawatts won't kill Snid – more's the pity – he's immortal; but they'll vaporise his apparatus and make him feel pretty sick for a time. And then *I'll* be hauled over the coals for infringing the Statute, I suppose. It's what you people call a Catch 22 situation.' She gazed grumpily around and her eyes fell on Mar Ten, who was now for some reason engaged in removing the offside front door of the car. 'I suppose it's no good asking sir over there if he'll condescend to tell the local goddess what he's up to?' she said loudly. The elf looked up, grinned and shook his head. Qenet sniffed disapprovingly. Josie considered that it was time to quieten things down a bit. 'How about walking up to the Sanctuary to see what's happening there?' she suggested. 'If the OHAG people did find the H-bomb and deliver it as planned last night it could be arriving at any time. Perhaps Qenet could have one last try at talking Snid out of his plans.'

'Some hopes,' muttered the goddess and sniffed again. 'But I suppose I'd better be around in case he decides to start pressing any buttons.' So the three of them, still rather depressed, tramped back up along the road towards Overton Hill.

Mar Ten remained alone on the site. By now he had taken the driver's seat out of the car and was replacing the fastening brackets with small electro-magnetic clamps. When he had checked these, he replaced the seat and walked back into Silbury, reappearing a little later accompanied by Rexy and carrying a small silver spheroid which he delicately placed on the floor of the car beneath the driver's seat. Next he unbolted the door hinges and replaced them with some more clamps. Then, leaving the dinosaur to watch the car, he once again disappeared into the hill and emerged carrying what appeared to be a thin six-foot roll of wire mesh. 'Shape-memory alloy,' he said softly as he flash-welded the edge of the roll to the bumper of the Citroën. 'Advanced technology for this sector – but it *has* been invented, so I'm not really breaking the rules, am I, Rexy?' There was no answering grunt, so he glanced up. But Rexy had vanished.

Not much seemed to be happening on Overton Hill. The towering drilling-rig, its work done, had disappeared, leaving only a deep shaft (carefully fenced off) and several sets of ridged track-marks gouged deeply into the soil. A few of the fencing panels that surrounded the western edge of the Sanctuary site had been removed – presumably to give the laser beam a clear path to its target inside the long barrow across the valley.

Looking towards West Kennett, Ben and Josie could just make out that the great centre blocking stone of the barrow's facade had been dragged out of its place and now rested at the downhill edge of the enclosure. The facade itself looked rather like a row of teeth with the middle one missing. Behind the gap, they knew, lay the access passage to the Transfer Station mechanism deep inside the ancient tomb. They knew, too, that in another sector of space-time something – or somebody – was already waiting for the right sequence of impulses to open the gatestone and allow entry into the world of the twentieth century.

Snid was there, too. He had set up a kind of command post on top of the round barrow by the Sanctuary. This gave him a view over both the bomb shaft (and the M.H.D. converter which by now had been assembled beside it) and the computer-linked laser in the Sanctuary. No doubt he could also see what was going on at the long barrow through the binoculars which hung around his neck.

Josie and Ben crept as near to the round barrow as they could. The Ridgeway, being a right of way, was still open, though their progress along it brought disapproving looks from the numerous Ministry of Ancient Monuments officials who were patrolling the area.

A long trench, crossed by a pair of heavy but unstable-looking concrete slabs, had been dug between the bomb shaft and the laser. At the bottom of it ran a thick, frost-covered pipe. A diesel generator was chugging away supplying power to a large and complicated pump with the words 'University of Salisbury. Department of Archaeology. Cryogenic (liquid hydrogen/helium) condenser. DO NOT APPROACH. HIGHLY DANGEROUS' stencilled upon it.

'Snid must be using superconducting cables to transmit power from the bomb to the laser,' whispered Ben. 'If he didn't keep the temperature as near to absolute zero as possible they would all blow like fuses when the current comes on.'

They were at the foot of Snid's barrow and could clearly see the elf above them as he picked up what must have been a portable radio transmitter and spoke into it, gazing as he did so towards the distant long barrow. 'Testing, testing,' he said loudly. 'Are you reading me, Krasnog? Is everything ready at your end?' He nodded as the reply came back, put the receiver down, and caught sight of Josie and Ben standing below him, an expression of shocked amazement on their faces. 'Shove off, you snotty little human

122

brats,' he shouted. 'Can't you see we're busy here?' They needed no
further urging. Utterly deflated, they made their way back across
the trench. The concrete slabs seemed to slip a little as they
crossed; almost subconsciously Josie noted that the side of the
excavation had been undercut at that point and looked as though it
might collapse at any moment. She hoped that it would; they
needed some luck, she reflected. If Krasnog had recovered so
quickly that he was well enough to supervise the work over at the
long barrow, the battle of the previous day on White Horse Hill had
all been in vain. They both felt slightly sick as they retailed the
news to Qenet, whose reaction showed her appreciation of human
psychology. 'Let's all go and get something to eat and drink,' she
said and led the way across the road to the café nearby.

The room was warm and cosy. It was still early for lunch and
only a few people had as yet come in. The good-looking dark girl
behind the counter recognised them at once. 'Hi there, handsome,'
she called out to Ben. 'What's it to be today? Chips with everything?' Qenet didn't give him a chance to reply. 'Give me some
crème-de-menthe, quick,' she commanded. 'No, a whole bottle,' she
added as the girl reached for a glass. And she marched off to a table
in the corner with all the purposefulness of a confirmed alcoholic.
The waitress cocked an amused and interrogative eyebrow at the
other two as they ordered their meals. 'Has something got up her
ladyship's nose this morning? Trouble with the lesser orders?' She
laughed, showing an unflawed set of teeth. Today she had plaited
reflective ribbon into her hair and this shone and sparkled as she
moved her head. She looked more like the lead singer from some
way-out group than a waitress in a café, thought Josie, impressed
by her exotic beauty and self-confident air.

They were not even able to complete their lunch without inter-
ruption. Qenet, unmindful of the curious looks she was attracting
from the other diners, drank half her liqueur straight from the
bottle, occasionally making rather theatrical remarks about the
shame and the shambles that had overtaken her. Ben and Josie
munched through their food without comment. Before they had
finished, however, the familiar roar of the OHAG crawler truck
made itself heard. Soon the enormous vehicle reached the crest of
the hill, turned in by the Sanctuary and inched its way once more
across the churned-up field towards the fence surrounding the
shaft. It no longer carried the drilling rig. Instead a large red
cylinder had been lashed to its loading platform. From where they
were sitting in the café the party could see a large painted skull
and crossbones and, underneath it, the inscription 'Danger. Explo-
sives. Do not drop'. Snid's H-bomb had arrived at its ground zero.

123

The three exchanged glances; things seemed to be going from bad to worse. Mar Ten's preparations for an elf-to-elf confrontation with Snid – whatever they were – would not be complete for several hours yet. Qenet took another long swig from her bottle. Thank goodness, reflected Josie, her metabolism was not affected by alcohol. 'Time to go and have a last try at making our Finky friend see reason,' said the goddess. 'Not that he'll take a blind bit of notice – he's too far gone already. But it's the least I can do before I give him the works.' She looked at Ben and Josie for agreement.

Josie had an idea. 'Suppose we could sabotage Snid's preparations for a few hours. That would at least give Mar Ten a chance. Tell me, Ben,' she turned towards her brother, 'what would happen if those cooling pipes were broken?'

Ben considered for a moment. 'I don't think Snid could detonate the bomb. If the cables weren't supercooled the current would probably melt them. But how can we stop the pump?' He brightened up. 'Put sugar in the fuel tank?'

'No, my idea's simpler than that,' said Josie. 'You must have noticed that the bridge thing over the trench is wobbly. One good jump on it and with any luck those slabs would give way. They look as though they weigh a ton and the sides of the trench are almost collapsing under the strain already.' She stood up. 'Come on, let's do some tap-dancing on Finky's helium pipes. I don't like being called a snotty brat, especially by a dude like him.'

Ben hesitated. 'That liquid helium's pretty hairy stuff, you know,' he began. 'Freeze you rock solid in a second. So we'd better be careful.' But he followed Josie outside. Together they crossed the road and walked down the Ridgeway track towards the trench. Nobody seemed to take much notice of them. Snid's command post on the round barrow was deserted and most of the attendants and workers were gathered round the shaft on the other side of the field.

They came to the excavation and gingerly crossed the bridge. The slabs seemed more stable this time; there was no give in them. Josie knelt down and pretended to do up a shoelace. She slipped her heel against the end of the concrete beam and pushed as hard as she could. Ben stood in front of her and gave an unobtrusive jump. The slab skidded forwards and sideways at the same moment. It collapsed with a satisfying crunch into the trench. Craning forward, they could see it resting against a length of insulated pipe. The lagging turned dark and began to steam as the liquid gas seeped through. They resumed their walk down towards East Kennett. Nobody followed them.

A quarter of an hour later they met Qenet, who had come down from Overton Hill to meet them as they returned along the road from the village. She seemed a good deal more cheerful. 'You certainly put the wind up Finky and his mob. He's just sent for the fire people.' She nodded towards the hilltop where several winking blue lights were visible. 'They've smothered half the field in foam. My friend Charlie says they reckon it'll be a couple of hours at least before the cryogenic pump can be started up again. Well done, noble warriors!' She held out her bottle. 'Have a swig. Things are looking up.'

The fire appliances stayed for over an hour. By the time that the liquid gas had evaporated and the foam had been hosed away it was late afternoon and the light was beginning to fade. A number of mobile floodlights had been rigged up by the Ministry of Ancient Monuments and at 4.30 they came on, giving a weird, almost lunar appearance to the muddy field.

Further off, across the valley, a group of lights winked on to show where Krasnog and his helpers were preparing the old Transfer Station for use once more. At five o'clock, in the gathering darkness, the clatter of the cryogenic pump started up again. Josie, who had been keeping watch by the lay-by, walked back to the café where Qenet and Ben were waiting. At the door she paused. The place was empty except for Qenet, Ben and the waitress. Qenet and Ben were gazing out across to the Sanctuary site; they looked tense and worried. The eyes of the waitress were focused in the same direction, and she was leaning with negligent grace against the counter. In one hand she was balancing a short silvery baton about two feet long. Perhaps she was a drum majorette in her spare time, reflected Josie as she hurried past – she certainly had the figure.

The other two stood up as Josie approached them. 'Time for the showdown with Finky,' said Qenet. 'Let's go and see if he'll respond to sweet reason. Otherwise I'll have to make the little jerk an offer he can't refuse.' Josie smiled inwardly. Qenet's language had changed perceptibly during the short time she had been in the twentieth century but she still couldn't differentiate between Queen's English and slang. The waitress grinned at them as they left. 'See you later, alligator,' she called out. 'After a while, crocodile,' immediately replied Josie, a long-term admirer of Bill Haley.

The three of them marched across the dark and deserted road. There was a kind of solemnity in the way in which they advanced, with Qenet slightly ahead and the other two flanking her like courtiers on a diplomatic mission. Already the goddess had slipped into an authoritative Mode 2 appearance. A Ministry of Ancient Monuments official stood at the Ridgeway gate. He peered at the approaching party. 'The track's closed,' he began. 'It's been diverted along the main road down to the East Kennett turn. . . .' His voice trailed away uncertainly.

'Snid,' said Qenet, as though she were mentioning something that wasn't very nice. 'Take me to Snid.' The man looked uncomfortable. 'I'm afraid I can't, madam,' he explained. 'The professor's very busy up there.' He gestured vaguely towards the round barrow.

'Snid,' repeated Qenet in a quiet voice. 'At once. Now. Pronto. Or I'll eviscerate you, buster.' She sounded as though she meant it. The man shuddered; he opened the gate and stood aside as they walked past him. They came to the bottom of the round barrow and climbed up its side.

Snid was sitting in a collapsible garden chair at the top. He was holding what appeared to be a small push-button radio. He waved affably. 'Hello, your ladyship,' he beamed. 'So you've brought your little human playmates to see the firework display, have you? How charming. Have a sandwich: smoked salmon – very good. Or is this more to your taste?' He picked up a bottle of champagne and a glass from the hamper beside him. 'You're all welcome to stay – though of course the radiation level around here's soon likely to be a little high for humans.' He sniggered.

Qenet ignored the invitation. She looked him straight in the eye and spoke slowly and deliberately, as though to a child. 'See here, Finky, you can't go ahead with this. You'd be tearing up the Statute – and you know it. No one ever gets away with that sort of thing. Sooner or later the Higher Powers will come and get you. You can't keep them out for ever, even with force-field isolators. They'll find you and grind you into a cloud of random quarks. They'll give you the black hole treatment. Remember the rule: Immortality is only absolute within the parameters of conventional physics. Now's your last chance to pull out, Snid. Otherwise your hour will come.'

For a moment Snid looked worried. Then his face cleared. 'Sorry, your ladyship. I've done the calculations. Tonight I'll force open the gatestone at Transfer Station I. I've got a Varang Slaver Mark VI telepathic controller waiting there to come through from the twenty-fifth century. It'll turn the humans here into a crowd of zombies. And it's equipped with a handy built-in 0·5 terawatt fusion plant. I'll replicate that and soon have sufficient FoFI power to take this whole benighted planet out of ambient space-time. And you with it, dearie. Now how about *you* reconsidering the offer I made to you at Salisbury the other day?'

With an effort Qenet kept her temper. 'Snid, you're no good at sums. You always get them wrong. That's why you're here now. All this thermonuclear equipment you've got here is incredibly primitive. It's a real lash-up. You'll never hit the right spatio-temporal co-ordinates. You'll goof again, sure as sure. So why not chuck it in before someone gets hurt?'

Snid shook his head and smiled. 'My dear Qenet, in a few minutes I shall press a red button here' – he indicated the transceiver in his hand – and detonate the tactical nuclear device over there. I would have done so some hours ago had not our cryogenic system unaccountably developed a leak.' He shifted his gaze to Josie and Ben. 'As it is, I'm only waiting for superconductivity to be established again. And then off we go. Excuse me.'

He pulled out the aerial of his radio, opened one of the channels, and spoke sharply. 'What's the cable temperature?' The reply was prompt. 'Two point five degrees up and falling steadily; ten more minutes should do it, sir.' Snid nodded. 'Prepare to evacuate site,' he ordered, and turned back to his visitors. 'Now to check on the Transfer Station. My faithful collaborator Krasnog should be standing by there. He's a little less than dainty in his habits and much better in a chariot than in a car – as perhaps you already know – but he's a dab hand with a battleaxe. He doesn't like you, Qenet. Not one little bit; and he would just love to get his own back on the young driver of a certain orange Citroën.' Snid looked mildly around, smiled again, changed channels and spoke once more into the radio. 'Krasnog – is all ready at your end?'

There was no reply. Snid frowned and bit his lip. 'Krasnog,' he fairly shouted, 'wake up, you lazy *muc*, will you. I've got some friends of yours here. Do you read me?'

There was silence again for a minute or two. Then a voice replied. After a few seconds Ben and Josie recognised it as that of Krasnog's ill-used assistant from Salisbury. He still sounded subdued. 'Professor Snid, sir,' he whispered. 'Slugwam here. Something's gone wrong. Horribly wrong. Over at the barrow, I mean Transfer Station. We've been attacked. Attacked by a – a – ' his voice broke, 'by a *dragon*, sir. A great green dragon. With enormous teeth. It came roaring out of the night about five minutes ago and went straight for Mr Krasnog. It dragged him off into the field and I think' – Slugwam paused again, evidently to nerve himself – 'I think it's *eating* him out there in the dark. . . .'

Snid cut him off in mid-sentence. He retuned the radio. 'Temperature?' he snapped. His fingers hovered over the red button. 'One degree above superconductivity. Give me another three or four minutes,' came the unemotional reply. The elf cursed unintelligibly and glared at the three in front of him. 'Dragon? Slugwam must be drunk; Krasnog too.' He pressed the button for Krasnog's channel. 'Will you answer, you barbaric oaf?' he bellowed. Silence. Then over the air, as if in defiant reply, came Rexy's spine-chilling roar.

Snid slowly lowered the transceiver. For the first time he seemed to realise that something had gone seriously wrong with his plans. He raised his head and looked at Qenet full in the face. 'A dinosaur. That's the hunting roar of a tyrannosaur. Only one person would be crazy enough to bring a dinosaur into this sector. Mar Ten. He's here somewhere.' Snid glanced around uneasily, almost as though he expected the elf to jump out at him from the shadows. Then he stiffened. Up on the Ridgeway the twin headlights of a car had come into sight. They swept up and down in great vertical arcs as the vehicle accelerated down the dead straight length of track leading to the Sanctuary. Already the distinctive howl of the Citroën's engine could be heard. The orange car came down the uneven and muddy track as though it were cruising along the outside lane of a motorway; it must have been travelling at well over fifty miles an hour as it burst into the illuminated area around the Sanctuary. The car careered across the road and there was time to see Mar Ten wave carelessly in their general direction as he skidded with shrieking tyres on to a collision course with the laser assembly.

The assortment of vehicles still parked in the lay-by seemed to form an impenetrable wall between the elf and his target. It looked as though the Citroën would flatten itself against one or the other of them. Then, only five yards or so before impact, something began to detach itself from the front bumper. A glittering mesh unrolled on to the nearest Range Rover to form a steep ramp from the road surface up to its roof. The car shot up the incline and, at the top, transformed itself into an airborne projectile. It hurtled over the fence and, descending in a neat curve, landed fair and square on the laser and the equipment which surrounded it in the middle of the Sanctuary. As the car impacted the offside door flew off. It was followed by a silvery force-field capsule which hit the earth and bounced off into the darkness like an enormous beach ball.

The group on top of the round barrow looked down at the twisted pile of scrap that, moments before, had been (by twentieth-century standards at least) a sophisticated piece of high-technology engineering. The laser and its ancillary computer could never be used again; individual components were scattered in various stages of fractured ruination across the Sanctuary site. The vehicle that had done all the damage had come to rest, relatively un-

128

scathed, at the far edge of the enclosure. Of Mar Ten there was no sign.

Something akin to anguish passed over Snid's face. He smiled in a quiet, half-resigned way as if acknowledging defeat. Then he raised his transceiver and pressed the red detonation button.

A violent impact swept Snid, Ben and Josie off their feet and sent them rolling down the side of the barrow. A thin haze of violet light flickered across the field and a miniature volcano of steam and smoke erupted from the bomb shaft. The earth around it began to glow a dull red; but there was no detonation, no blinding flash.

Qenet was standing alone on the round barrow facing the bomb. Her hands were extended as though to attract its force. Vast quantities of energy were streaming into her body; the radiant green of her dress and the brightness of her arms and face lit up the whole area as she strove to absorb the power of the nuclear explosion that Snid had triggered off. The scene had a static quality about it which was broken only by the hissing of what by now was the lava field around the shaft and by the auroral shimmer which danced around the figure of the goddess.

Then the stars began to go out one by one. The molten chalk slowly congealed. Again there was that feeling of isolation from time and space which Ben and Josie had first experienced in the stone circle at Mitchell's Fold. They were once more in a stasis field.

'Hold it, funsters, the game's over,' cried a good-humoured and familiar voice. 'You can switch off the fairy lights, lady – you've stopped that neutron flux like it's lead. The stuff in that bomb wouldn't raise a click on a geiger in a hundred years.'

The darkness cleared. Three new faces were visible just inside the edge of the field: Mar Ten, rather tousled and muddy; T. Rexy, muddy and looking rather pleased with himself and, in front of them, the waitress from the café, dark and immaculate in her red velvet outfit. It was she who had spoken. She still held her short silvery stick in her left hand and she was smiling amiably. 'Sorry to gatecrash the party. Allow me to introduce myself in my new persona. Alecto's the name, retribution's the game. I'm your friendly neighbourhood Fury. Meg, Tizzy and I felt that the old snake's-hair image was getting altogether too trad so we updated it. And how do you like our new-style neutrino-deactivators?'

She held up her rod and the other three immortals each took a sharp step backwards. 'When I discovered that three non-humans had suddenly made a bee-line for this forsaken sector of space-time I simply had to come along and join the fun. Hope you don't mind.'

She turned to Snid and the smile died from her eyes. There was a

129

subdued 'pop' and a large black bubble materialised at the end of her rod. Alecto now spoke in a hard voice. 'Snid, you have repeatedly broken the Statute despite warnings from the area goddess. You have sought to rule humans through force and – worse – by the use of temporal anomaly. You have also taken active measures to extract this sector from the continuum and to control it for your own perverted ends. All this is incontestable. You must go. Now!'

The black sphere detached itself from Alecto's rod and floated gently towards Snid. Suddenly the elf seemed to become smaller. Or perhaps the black hole became larger – it was difficult to tell. Snid appeared to fade and lose substance. The outline of the round barrow behind him slowly became visible through his body. His appearance took on the immobility of a holographic image.

Alecto withdrew her rod and the black hole vanished at once. Snid's image remained suspended in the air, ghost-like and transparent. The Fury stepped forward and passed her hand through the spectre. 'It's the event horizon effect,' she explained matter-of-factly. 'The black hole stabilises the light rays from the objects it absorbs. I wonder what Snid will get up to in his new dimension. It's the ultimate cosmic sin-bin down there. All the immortal gangsters of the last thirteen billion years.'

Qenet sat down on the barrow; she seemed tired. 'I suppose there will have to be an erase and re-run.'

Alecto nodded. 'I guess so. We'll probably get away with a localised one for the solar system only. That'll mean winding time back to the day you first made contact with your human friends here.' She grinned at Josie and Ben. 'No doubt a few astronomers will notice that pulsars and variable stars have jumped out of phase but no one will take much notice of *them*. We can't leave things as they are. Your pyrotechnic display tonight – to say nothing of Mar Ten's sensational death-defying ride and Rexy's little picnic over at West Kennett – will have been seen by far too many people. A re-run is the only way out.'

Alecto faced Josie and Ben. 'I expect you understood the gist of that, didn't you? I'm sorry we've got to erase the last nine days – it's probably been quite an experience for you. But, you see, there's no real alternative. If poor old Finky hadn't tried to detonate his damned bomb, I expect her ladyship, Mar Ten and even Rexy could have kept a low profile and transferred back the normal way. But in the circumstances I'm afraid we've simply got to wipe out this evening's rave-up and the events leading to it.'

She stood to attention. With a strange, almost old-world formality Qenet, Mar Ten and Rexy ranged themselves in a line beside her. Josie and Ben shook each in turn by the hand.

'Thanks for the help, kiddos,' said Alecto. 'We'd have been in real trouble without you.'

'I'll be back' said Qenet. 'This crummy sector of space-time needs a goddess to look after it. See you next Samain.'

'Me too,' said Mar Ten. 'Your internal combustion engines have intriguing possibilities. I'd like to give that car of yours a real overhaul.'

And Rexy winked.

DAY ONE

It was a dull wet autumn afternoon. The school bus swung across the A 4 road into a lay-by, skidded slightly and bounced off the kerb before stopping. The schoolchildren got out; most of them made for Silbury Hill, a couple of hundred yards up the road. Ben, with two illicit cans of pale ale in his anorak pockets, made for the West Kennett long barrow. Soon he was joined by his sister. As they plodded up the hill Josie unzipped the centre pocket of her anorak, pulled out her radio-cassette and switched on. Radio 1 blared out over the peaceful dampness of the countryside. One of the interminable request programmes was on.

They reached the massive stone facade of the long barrow and sat down by the entrance. The disc-jockey's voice came over loud and clear: 'And next we have a top-priority special request for Josie and Ben of the Old Station, West Kennett, near Silbury, Wiltshire. A real old schmaltzy number for you, straight from World War Two, with love and best wishes from your friends Martin, Rexy and her ladyship – now who – who – who might that be? Anyway, off we go. . . .' Ben and Josie gazed at each other in astonishment as the unfamiliar words and music increased in volume:

> We'll meet again,
> Don't know where,
> Don't know when,
> But I know we'll meet again
> Some sunny day. . . .

Josie looked at Ben; Ben looked at Josie. 'You know,' he said, 'I think we've been here before.'

079506 94119

COMPTON
BEAUCHAMP

PORT WAY

WAYLAND'S SMITHY

RIDGE

WA

WO

To Ashbury